MANDIE®
AND THE
HIDDEN PAST

Mandie® Mysteries

MANDIE®
AND THE
HIDDEN PAST

Lois Gladys Leppard

BETHANY HOUSE PUBLISHERS
MINNEAPOLIS, MINNESOTA 55438

Published by Bethany House Publishers
11400 Hampshire Avenue South
Bloomington, Minnesota 55438
www.bethanyhouse.com

Bethany House Publishers is a Division of
Baker Book House Company, Grand Rapids, Michigan.

Printed in the United States of America

ISBN 0-7642-2641-X

With love to a special little reader—
KAHLA ERICKSON

About the Author

LOIS GLADYS LEPPARD worked in Federal Intelligence for thirteen years in various countries around the world. She now makes her home in South Carolina.

The stories of her mother's childhood as an orphan in western North Carolina are the basis for many of the incidents incorporated into this series.

Visit her Web site: *www.Mandie.com*.

Contents

"Trust no future, howe'er pleasant!
Let the dead Past bury its dead!
Act, act in the living present!
Heart within, and God o'erhead!"

—HENRY WADSWORTH LONGFELLOW

Chapter 1 / Home Again

"Let's walk to the house," Mandie told her friends as everyone stood on the depot platform.

John Shaw overheard this remark and said, "That would save Abraham and Mr. Bond from having to make two trips for us and our luggage."

"Yes, sir," Mandie said with a smile, holding on to Snowball's red leash and looking at Celia, Joe, and Jonathan.

They had all just arrived in Franklin, North Carolina, from the Pattons' house in Charleston, South Carolina. And the adults, John Shaw and Elizabeth, Mrs. Taft and Senator Morton, Lindall Guyer and Celia Hamilton's mother, Jane, and Uncle Ned, would be able to squeeze into the Shaws' rig, which Mr. Bond had brought to the depot to pick them up. Abraham was driving the Shaws' wagon, and it would be filled with trunks and other baggage.

Joe looked at Mandie, smiled, and said, "I imagine you have a reason for offering to walk."

Mandie wasn't about to reveal that reason, either. She was anxious to get to the Shaws' house ahead of the adults so she could get into the secret tunnel to inspect the crack in the wall, which Uncle Ned had come to Charleston to tell John Shaw about.

"Come on, let's go," Mandie said to her friends.

"Amanda," Elizabeth Shaw called to her, "no stops along the way. Go straight home."

"Yes, ma'am, we'll hurry," Mandie replied with a grin as she looked at Joe.

The young people hastened down the street from the depot. Mandie set the pace, and she was in a hurry. Even Jonathan, a New Yorker used to fast walking, had trouble keeping up with her.

"Mandie, do you have to walk so fast?" Jonathan asked as he kept by her side.

Mandie slowed just a little to look at him as she replied, "I can't explain right now, but I want to get to the house before my mother and the others do. So we have to hurry." She walked even faster.

"I think you should go on ahead and we'll catch up with you," Celia said, blowing out her breath.

"That's a good idea," Joe agreed, slowing down to Celia's side.

Mandie glanced back and said, "All right, y'all know the way to my house." With that remark, she started practically running down the street. Jonathan, however, stayed right with her, determined not to let her get ahead. At the next corner Mandie and Jonathan cut through a back street, while Joe and Celia continued down the main thoroughfare. Snowball forged ahead at the end of his leash.

Within ten minutes, Mandie was opening the gate to the long walkway in front of the Shaws' house.

Between gasps for breath, she said, "I hope no one sees us come in."

Jonathan, close by her side, asked as he, too, tried to get his breath, "Why do you not want anyone to see us?"

"Just because I don't," Mandie managed to say. She picked up her long skirts and ran up the front steps onto the long veranda. Pulling open the screen door, she quickly unfastened Snowball's leash and let him run ahead down the main hall.

"Let's go upstairs to Uncle John's office," she told Jonathan as she hurried for the main staircase.

Suddenly Aunt Lou, the housekeeper, came hurrying toward them from the back hall. "I knowed my chile be home when dat white cat showed up," the old woman was saying with a big smile.

"Oh, shucks!" Mandie said under her breath to Jonathan.

As Aunt Lou caught up with them, she said, "I see you done brought dat Yankee boy home wid you." She reached for Mandie and gave her a quick hug.

"Yes, ma'am, I'm that Yankee boy come to visit awhile," Jonathan said with a big grin as the woman patted him on the shoulder.

"The rig wouldn't hold all of us, so we walked," Mandie explained. "So did Joe and Celia, but we were in a hurry and left them behind." She was about to explain to Aunt Lou the reason she had rushed ahead of the others when Liza, the young maid, came rushing down the hallway to greet them.

"Oh, Missy 'Manda, I'se right glad you got home 'fo' dis heah house fall down," Liza said. She danced around the hallway.

"Liza, hush yo' mouth," Aunt Lou said. "Ain't nuthin' but a li'l crack in de wall downstairs. Ain't about to fall in." Turning back to Mandie, she asked, "Who all be comin' wid you?"

"Everyone," Mandie said. "Joe, Celia and her mother, Grandmother and Senator Morton,

Jonathan's father, and Uncle Ned. And my mother and Uncle John, of course. We all came home so Uncle John could have something done about that crack. And I was glad to leave the Pattons' house because so many strange things kept happening."

"What kinda strange thangs?" Liza asked as she stood still and looked at Mandie.

"I'll tell you about it later, Liza. Right now I want to go down and see the crack in the wall of the tunnel before everyone else gets here," Mandie said.

"So that's why you were practically running all the way home," Jonathan said with a big grin.

"Cain't see de crack," Liza said. "Mistuh Jason Bond he locked de do' and totes de key wid him."

Mandie was surprised. "Why does he do that?" she asked.

"So's dat if part of de house fall in de other part won't," Liza said. "Or sumpin' like dat, I guess."

Mandie and Jonathan smiled at the girl.

Aunt Lou scolded Liza. "Liza, git back in de kitchen and git dem potatoes peeled," she said, shaking her large white apron at the girl.

Liza quickly started down the hallway toward the kitchen door. She turned back to say, "When y'all git to see dat crack, don't stay in there too long. Might fall in."

"All right, Liza," Mandie replied as the girl opened the kitchen door. Looking at Aunt Lou, Mandie asked, "Did Mr. Bond really lock the tunnel up?"

"Dat he did, my chile, till we sees if it be dangerous," the old woman replied. "Now dat Mistuh John come home we find out."

Joe Woodard and Celia Hamilton came in the front door and down the hallway to join them.

"Glad you young'uns got here safe. Now I has to

go see 'bout de food," Aunt Lou greeted Joe and Celia. As she started toward the kitchen door, she looked back and smiled as she said, "I do believe Jenny's bakin' a cake, a chocolate one."

"But you didn't know I was coming," Joe teased.

"No matter, I knows all you young'uns like chocolate cake," she replied and disappeared into the kitchen.

Mandie explained to Joe and Celia why she was in such a hurry to get home as they all sat down on the bottom step of the huge staircase. "And now I find out Mr. Jason has it locked up and I can't get into the tunnel," she added with a sigh.

The kitchen door opened down the hallway, and Liza stepped out and called to them, "Abraham, he be in de backyard wid de luggage. Say he need help."

Joe and Jonathan quickly rose and started for the kitchen door. Mandie and Celia followed.

The boys helped carry in the trunks and put them in the appropriate rooms. The girls brought in the handbags and smaller things.

As they came inside with the last load, Mandie said, "Let's all go to our rooms and get cleaned up. Mother and the others ought to be here shortly."

"They must have taken a detour," Joe remarked as they all started for the staircase.

"Yes, Abraham said my father had to see to his railcar being put on the side rail, and then he wanted to go by one of the stores," Jonathan explained.

"I'll see y'all back down here by the steps in ten minutes," Mandie told the boys as they climbed the steps.

"Ten minutes? I don't believe two girls can get changed that fast," Jonathan teased.

Joe grinned at him and said loudly, "It all depends on what they are planning to do."

Mandie, a few steps above the boys, paused to look down on them and said, "You know very well what I am planning to do. I'm going to see the crack in the tunnel as soon as it is possible."

Everyone laughed and continued up the stairs and to their rooms.

Mandie and Celia quickly opened their trunks, hung up their dresses, and then changed clothes.

As she was buttoning up the front of her gingham dress, Mandie said suddenly, "Oh, Celia, I'm wondering if the outside entrance to the tunnel is locked. Do you want to go with me to find out? I'd only take a couple of minutes." She finished the last button and hurried to the bureau to brush back her long blond hair. She tied it back with a ribbon to match her red dress.

Celia tied her sash around her waist and smoothed the full skirt of her green dress. "But, Mandie, even if it is open we wouldn't have time to go into the tunnel. Your mother and the others will be here any minute," she replied.

Mandie started for the door. "Come on, Celia," she said as she opened the door. "If you don't want to go with me, I'll go by myself."

Celia, following, reluctantly agreed. "Well, all right, but we'll have to practically run down there and back."

Joe and Jonathan were waiting by the staircase. Jonathan pulled out his pocket watch, opened the cover, and said, "Nine minutes. You made it."

"And you can be sure they are up to something," Joe said teasingly.

"We're going to see if the outside entrance to the

tunnel is locked," Mandie replied, going on down the hallway toward the back door.

"I was wondering when you would think about that," Joe teased as he and Jonathan followed the girls out the back door.

They hurried down the hill, through the trees, to a secret door that opened into the tunnel. Mandie got there first and gave a push on the door. It opened so suddenly she almost fell inside.

"It's unlocked," she exclaimed as she got her balance and tried to see into the tunnel.

"Yes, but I don't see any lanterns around here, and you know very well it is too dark to see your hand in front of your face in that tunnel," Joe reminded her as he and the others stopped outside the door.

"Oh, shucks!" Mandie exclaimed, stomping her foot as she stood just inside the doorway. "We can go back and get a lantern," she decided and came outside in a hurry.

"We do not have time for that, Mandie," Celia said.

Mandie turned to start back up the hill. "Maybe if we hurry," she said and began practically running, holding up the skirt of her dress.

When they arrived at the back door they were all out of breath.

Jonathan collapsed on the steps and said, "Whew! I'm not used to such fast living."

Celia stopped to lean against the rail around the back porch.

Joe plopped down beside Jonathan and said, "Neither am I."

"I'll be right back. I'll get a lantern out of the

pantry," Mandie told them as she went on inside the back door.

"Oh, shucks!" Mandie whispered to herself as she saw the front door open at the other end of the hall. Her mother and all the other adults came inside. She didn't have time to get the lantern and go back to the tunnel entrance.

Jonathan, Joe, and Celia came in the back door.

"I don't believe we can go back down there right now," Joe said to Mandie as they watched the adults go into the parlor at the front of the hall.

"You are right," Mandie agreed, blowing out her breath.

"Let's have a conference," Jonathan said, leading the way to the staircase, where he and Joe sat on the bottom step and the girls sat on the bench by the stairs.

"It seems we have to make other plans," Joe said.

"I don't think they will stay in the parlor long, because they will want to change clothes after that long train ride," Celia remarked.

Liza came out of the kitchen. She was rolling the tea cart, and as she passed them, she said, "Miz Lizbeth she tell Mistuh Bond to tell Aunt Lou to tell me to bring de coffee to de parlor. I'se jes' sayin' dis jes' in case y'all want some." She grinned as she went on toward the parlor.

"She didn't say what she had to eat on that cart," Joe said with a big grin.

"Let's just go and find out," Jonathan said as he stood up.

"That's a good idea," Celia said, also rising.

Mandie stood up and said, "Hope it's chocolate cake." She grinned at her friends as they all hurried down the hallway to the parlor.

The adults were busy with their own conversation. The young people sat on the other side of the parlor and waited for Liza to finish with the others.

As Liza rolled the cart over to them, she smiled and said, "I knowed y'all gwine come after me. I sho' did. Ain't got no choc'late cake on heah, but we sho' got some good choc'late cookies." She winked at them and added, "I knows 'cause I done et one."

Mandie and her friends laughed and helped themselves to the coffee and chocolate cookies.

"Now I has to put dis heah cart back over dere near Miz Lizbeth 'cause Aunt Lou said so, and I has to go back and help wid de food," Liza told them. She rolled the cart to the other side of the room and then passed by the young people on her way out. "Don't y'all eat too many of dem cookies," she said. "Save some room for dat choc'late cake what we's gwine have fo' supper." She hurried out into the hallway.

Joe looked at the others, grinned, and said, "Well, now we know what we're going to have for supper—chocolate cake."

"Yes," Jonathan responded.

Mandie tried to listen to the adults' conversation on the other side of the room, but as far as she could tell, they weren't discussing the crack in the tunnel. They were talking about their visit with the Pattons in Charleston.

Then in a few minutes, Mrs. Taft stood up and said, "I need to go to my room and rest a little before supper."

Jane Hamilton rose from her chair and said, "And I need to clean up and change clothes."

All the other adults also stood up and prepared

to leave the parlor. Mandie decided to speak to Uncle John. She hurried to catch him as he started toward the door to the hall. He was talking to Lindall Guyer, and Mandie had to step in front of him to get his attention.

"Uncle John, could I—" she began to ask, when he quickly interrupted.

"The answer is no, Amanda," John Shaw said. "I know your curiosity has got the best of you, but you will not be allowed in the tunnel until I have inspected the crack and decided what to do about it."

As he walked on, Mandie quickly said, "But couldn't I—"

"I said no, Amanda," John Shaw firmly told her. "Now, I don't want to hear any more about it. I'll let you know when you may go into the tunnel." He quickly followed the other adults out of the room.

Mandie just stood there and stomped her foot. "I don't see why I can't go into the tunnel with him," she mumbled to herself as she walked back across the room to her friends.

"If that crack caused the support beams to shift or break, it really could be dangerous, Mandie," Joe told her as she sat down.

"Your uncle is thinking of your safety," Jonathan added.

"Well, if that crack is dangerous, then, just like Liza said, the house could fall in," Mandie grumbled. "But we are all in the house."

"Remember, Mandie, Uncle Ned has seen the crack, and he has probably told your uncle John how bad it is," Celia reminded her.

"I imagine that's where all the men have gone right now," Mandie said. "Therefore, I can't get the lantern and go in from the outside entrance to see the crack."

Joe frowned at her and said, "Mandie, you are not planning on going into that tunnel before your uncle gives you permission to, are you? Remember, he said you were not to go into the tunnel until he said you could."

Mandie blew out her breath and rose and walked around the room. "I know what he said. But what difference would it make if I went in from the outside entrance? No one would really know it," she argued.

"Mandie! Mandie!" Celia exclaimed. "You are talking about disobeying him. You know you shouldn't do that."

Mandie looked at her and didn't reply as she continued walking about the room.

"This is one mystery that I refuse to take part in," Jonathan said. "I certainly don't want to get in trouble with your uncle."

"Neither will I," Celia said.

"Remember what Uncle Ned always tells you: think before you act," Joe reminded her.

"All right, all right, we won't talk about it any more," Mandie quickly told him. Taking a deep breath, Mandie straightened up and headed for the door. "I'm going to my room to rest until it's time for supper. I'll see y'all then." She quickly went out into the hallway.

She mumbled to herself as she went up the staircase two steps at a time. None of her friends said anything, and none of them followed her.

"That's all right," she said to herself. "I'll find a way to get to see the crack."

The door to her room was partly open, and she found Snowball curled up in the middle of her bed.

She reached for his leash and gave him a push to wake him up.

"Come on, Snowball, let's go outside," she told the cat.

Snowball meowed and sat up to wash his face.

She fastened on his leash but picked him up and carried him down the hall to the back stairs. No one was in sight as she pushed open the back door and went outside.

She walked around the back of the house and went down the hill to the creek, where the old house had stood that was blown away by the tornado in the spring.

Snowball pulled forward on his leash and managed to get to the edge of the water, where minnows were swimming around. He stuck a paw in the creek and tried to catch one. He got excited as the minnows quickly evaded him.

Mandie sat down on a huge boulder at the edge of the water and watched the cat. She thought about what had transpired in the parlor and realized she had been very rude with her friends. She would have to ask their forgiveness. She was truly sorry about that, but she wouldn't change her mind about finding a way to see the crack in the tunnel. Somehow she would accomplish that.

Chapter 2 / A Tiring Day

Mandie reentered the house through the back door. She removed Snowball's leash and set him down. He raced down the hallway out of sight. She walked on down to the parlor door and looked into the room. All her friends were still there, quietly talking among themselves, but she could not understand what they were talking about.

Suddenly Joe looked up and saw her in the doorway. He grinned at her and said, "That was a quick rest. We were just trying to decide whether we should go for a walk." He stood up. "Come on in," he added and then teasingly said, "We might even let you go with us."

Mandie felt tears come into her blue eyes and quickly took a few deep breaths before she entered the parlor and replied, "I appreciate the friendship of all of you. And I apologize for my rude behavior. I am sorry from the bottom of my heart. Will y'all forgive me?" She stood in the middle of the room as she looked at each one.

Everyone tried to talk at one time.

"You don't have to apologize to me for anything, Mandie," Celia quickly said. "We are all tired after that long trip."

"She is right," Jonathan agreed. "We are all a little out of sorts."

"And you know that includes me," Joe said. "Now come on, let's all go outside."

"We can't go far. It's almost time for supper," Mandie reminded him.

"We could go sit in the rose arbor. They must be blooming now and would smell so good," Celia suggested.

"Yes, the roses are blooming," Mandie said.

"Then, let's go," Joe said, leading the way out of the parlor and out the back door.

As they walked down the hill toward the rose arbor, Mandie was surprised to see her uncle John, Jonathan's father, and Uncle Ned coming up the hill.

"Look, there's Uncle John coming from down toward the creek." Mandie stopped to look ahead as she spoke to her friends. "And Uncle Ned and your father, Jonathan."

"And they are carrying lanterns," Jonathan said.

"Which means they probably came out of the outside entrance to the tunnel," Joe added.

"Yes," Mandie agreed.

The young people waited until the men came up to where they were standing on the pathway.

"That is some tunnel. I hadn't been all the way through it before," Lindall Guyer told his son, Jonathan.

"Yes, sir, it is," Jonathan agreed. "It must have taken a lot of time and work."

"My father had it built, you know," John Shaw explained to Jonathan. "I always think of how many Cherokee people were saved from the white soldiers, who were slaughtering every Indian they could find during the Removal."

"Yes, your father saved many Cherokee lives," Uncle Ned added.

"Is the crack dangerous, Uncle John?" Mandie quickly asked.

"We are not sure yet. We need to do a little more investigating," John Shaw told her. "We'll let y'all know when you can go in the tunnel and look at it. Now we've got to get cleaned up for supper." He started to walk on, and the other two men followed.

"Come on," Celia said, going ahead. "I've got to at least smell the roses."

"I can smell them from here," Jonathan said as they all began following Celia down the hill.

When they came within sight of the arbor, they all stopped to gaze at the beautiful climbing pink roses adorning the framework.

"Oh, how beautiful!" Celia said with a loud intake of breath.

"I believe roses are my favorite flowers," Joe remarked as he went toward the blooming mass and bent to smell the flowers.

"Roses are beautiful, but I prefer pansies," Jonathan said. "They are small and dainty and orderly."

"And they won't stick you," Mandie added with a smile.

"Well, if you don't touch the roses, they won't stick you, either," Celia argued.

Mandie was still thinking of the crack in the tunnel and wondering how she could get inside to see it. Since Uncle John and the others had come out from the outside entrance, she was pretty sure they had locked the door. So now both ends of the tunnel were locked up. She would have to find a way to check the entrances, and she didn't want to discuss the tunnel anymore with her friends. She would have to explore alone.

Suddenly she wondered how long her friends would be here. Looking at Joe, she asked, "Is your father coming to get you?"

"He had said he would be making calls around this area and would check to see when I got back from Charleston with y'all," Joe explained. He sat down on the bench under the arbor, and the others joined him.

"Since our plans got changed and we didn't stop off to see Lily on our way back here, I don't know when my mother will want to go home," Celia said.

"It would have been nice seeing Lily," Jonathan said. "But I know your uncle was worried about that crack in the tunnel, so it's better we came straight back here, Mandie. However, I do know my father has to get back to work in a day or two."

"A day or two?" Mandie asked. "Maybe he'll let you stay a few more days with us. We do have quite a bit of our vacation time still left."

"Just think, this is our last vacation from school, Mandie. Next summer we will be graduating," Celia said.

"Yes, and then going to college," Mandie said. "And we've got to decide which college we are going to soon."

"And that is going to be a problem," Celia said. "What if we don't agree on the same college?"

"The same college? Celia Hamilton, you have to go to the same college with me," Mandie quickly told her.

"Why don't you both just come down to New Orleans to the college where I go?" Joe asked.

"No, come up to New York to college with me," Jonathan quickly said.

Mandie glanced up the hill and saw Liza hurrying down it.

"Suppertime! Suppertime!" Liza was screaming.

Everyone stood up as she approached.

"We heard you," Mandie yelled back at the girl. "We're coming right now."

"Miz Lizbeth say to make it quick," Liza told her as she came to stand by the arbor.

"All right, Liza. How about going back and telling her we're on the way?" Mandie said.

Liza started back and then stopped, looked at Mandie, and said, "Bettuh hurry. Dey talkin' 'bout dat crack."

"All right, we'll hurry," Mandie said, glancing at her friends as she started up the hill behind Liza.

The young people went straight to the parlor, where Mandie knew everyone gathered before a meal. They silently entered the room and found seats as near the adults as possible.

John Shaw was saying, "I don't want to bring in any local help to repair the crack because I don't want outsiders going into the tunnel. It has always been kept private. There are still people around today who would frown on the fact that my father built it just to protect his Cherokee friends."

"I'm sure we men here could do the work," Lindall Guyer said.

"But don't you have to get back to New York in a day or two?" John Shaw asked.

Lindall Guyer glanced at his son, Jonathan, and then back at John Shaw and said, "I can take a few days longer. I'll just have to send a message to New York."

"That's fine. I appreciate that," John Shaw said.

Senator Morton, sitting by Mrs. Taft nearby, said, "John, you know I'm an old hand at repairing concrete since I'm from Florida, where we have lots of that kind of structure. I'd certainly be glad to pitch in and help. And I'm in no hurry to leave here."

"That's very kind of you, Senator," John Shaw said. "We can certainly use your knowledge on this."

Mandie leaned toward her friends on the settee and whispered, "Seems no one is going home any time soon."

"As soon as this other man Uncle Ned has contacted comes to take a look, we'll see what can be done to close the crack," John Shaw said.

Liza came to the doorway and announced loudly, "Miz Lizbeth, de supper be on de table." And she quickly went on down the hallway.

"Shall we go eat?" Elizabeth Shaw said, rising from her chair.

"Don't forget we're going to have chocolate cake," Joe whispered to the other young people as they followed the adults into the dining room.

"Yes," Mandie said.

The young people were seated together at one end of the long table, with the adults at the other end. Therefore, private conversations could be carried on by either group. Sometimes Mandie was glad for this opportunity to talk to her friends, but at other times she was frustrated because she couldn't hear what was being said at the other end of the table.

She tried to listen in on the adults' discussion of the crack in the secret tunnel but couldn't hear enough of anything to know what they were saying. She wondered if Uncle John had asked the adults to keep the information on the crack confidential.

"Why are you so quiet, Mandie? What are you thinking about?" Celia asked.

"It's easy to know what she's thinking about. The crack in the tunnel, of course," Joe said teasingly.

Mandie laid down her fork, looked at each of her friends, and said, "I am quiet because I am trying to hear what Uncle John is talking about. And so far I haven't been able to understand a thing that is being said. I believe the people at that end of the table are in a conspiracy of some kind."

Her friends all laughed. Mandie ignored them as she tried to concentrate on the discussion at the other end of the table. However, she was not able to pick up a single bit of conversation. So she decided to follow them into the parlor when the meal was over.

As everyone rose from the table later, Mandie turned to her friends and said, "I know, of course, that we had the chocolate cake here at the table tonight, but I thought we might go into the parlor for a little while and find out if there is any more information on the crack in the tunnel." Then, looking at the three, she added, "Of course, if y'all had rather do something else, we can."

"Oh no," Jonathan said.

"Whatever you want to do is fine with me," Joe said.

"Me too, Mandie," Celia added.

Mandie smiled at them and led the way behind the adults to the parlor. After everyone was seated, Liza brought coffee on the tea cart, but the young people didn't take any. And the adults seemed to have nothing to talk about but their visit to the Pattons.

Finally Mandie straightened up in her chair and said to her friends, "If there is anything else y'all would like to do, we could do it, whatever. I don't think they are even going to mention the tunnel." She blew out her breath.

"Well," began Celia, "we could—" she stopped as John Shaw spoke.

"Now, the man to inspect the tunnel should be here tomorrow, and then we can decide on a schedule for repairs," John Shaw was saying to the other men.

"Then I won't send the message to my office until we figure out how long I should stay to help with the work," Lindall Guyer replied.

At that moment Mandie heard a loud knock on the front door, which was just outside the parlor at the end of the hallway. She looked at her friends and said, "I wonder who that is."

They could hear Liza answering the door, and she was saying, "Dey all be in de parlor."

Mandie heard their next-door neighbor, Mrs. Cornwallis, reply, "Thank you, Liza. We'll just go right in."

"Oh no!" Mandie muttered under her breath. The visitors were Mrs. Cornwallis and her daughter, Polly, who always seemed to chase after Joe when he was visiting the Shaws.

Mrs. Cornwallis and Polly appeared in the doorway. Elizabeth Shaw saw them and rose to say, "Y'all come right in."

The men all rose to speak and then sat back down.

"We thought we'd just drop in for a few minutes," Mrs. Cornwallis said as she took a seat near the men. "We heard that Mr. Guyer and Jane Hamilton were here. I do hope we are not interrupting any-thing."

"Oh no, of course not," Elizabeth Shaw replied.

Then Polly found a seat between Jonathan and Joe. "Did y'all have a nice visit in Charleston with the Pattons?" she asked, looking around the group.

Mandie didn't reply. Celia, however, looked at the girl and said with a smile, "Of course. We always do when we go to their house."

"Where have you been since school let out for the summer?" Mandie asked the girl.

"Mother and I went to Atlanta to see some friends," Polly replied. Then turning to Joe, she asked, "How long are you going to be here?"

Joe frowned as he replied, "I'm not sure. I have to wait for my father."

"It must be awfully inconvenient having a doctor for a father and never being able to keep a schedule because of his calls," Polly replied, smiling at Joe and tossing back her long dark hair.

"No, it isn't inconvenient for me. I'm used to it, and I'm proud of my father being a doctor and help-ing sick people," Joe said with a little smile.

"But you are not going to be a doctor," Polly said. "At least, the last time I heard, you weren't."

"No, I am not," Joe answered.

"Are you staying home the rest of the summer?" Mandie asked. She wanted to know in order to try to avoid the girl. Polly usually caused trouble and was very inquisitive about other people's affairs.

"I think so, but I am not positive yet," Polly said. "Mother and I may go to New York to shop." Turning to Jonathan, she asked, "When are you and your father going home to New York?"

"I have no idea. My father will decide that," Jonathan replied.

"The Shaws' cook told our cook that y'all were here, and we thought we'd come over and find out if you would be home in New York in a few days, just in case we go up there," Polly said.

"Like I said, I do not know," Jonathan repeated.

"Have you decided what college you will be going to when we graduate next spring?" Celia asked.

"Mother has decided that we should go down and look at the one Joe goes to in New Orleans and then to New York to look at one there," Polly replied. "Where are you and Mandie going?"

"We don't know yet. We have not come to an agreement, and therefore we may go to different colleges," Celia said.

Mandie quickly said, "Oh no, Celia. We are going to the same college, somewhere."

"But we haven't come up with a mutually agreeable place," Celia said.

"We will soon," Mandie insisted. "I am not going to a college where I don't know a single soul. I remember how awful it was when I started at the Heathwoods' school because I had no friends there, and then I met you." She was trying to listen to the adults' conversation while they talked, and as far as she could tell, her uncle had not mentioned the crack in the tunnel to Mrs. Cornwallis. He knew how the lady and her daughter could meddle in other people's affairs.

"Did y'all buy anything in Charleston while y'all were at the Pattons' house?" Polly asked, glancing at all of the young people.

"We didn't go shopping, no," Mandie replied.

"I picked up a couple of shells down by the water," Jonathan said.

Mandie was relieved to see Mrs. Cornwallis rise from her chair. They were going home. Polly also stood up.

"We have to go now," Polly said. "Will y'all be home tomorrow? I could come back."

"I have no idea as to what we will be doing tomorrow, Polly," Mandie said. "But you could come back over and see." She added this last remark for fear of being too abrupt with the girl, but she hoped Polly would find somewhere else to go.

As soon as Mrs. Cornwallis and Polly left, with Elizabeth seeing them out the front door, John Shaw looked across the parlor at the young people and said, "I didn't have time to warn you all, but I don't want anyone outside this house to know about the crack in the tunnel. This is a private family matter, and I want to keep it that way."

"I didn't mention it," Mandie quickly told him.

"Neither did I," Joe said.

"And I didn't, either. That girl, Polly, asks so many questions you wouldn't have time to tell her anything," Jonathan said with a big grin.

"I didn't say anything about it, either," Celia said.

"That's good," John Shaw said.

"Uncle John, do you know yet what time the man will come tomorrow to look at the crack?" Mandie asked.

"No, I do not," he said. "And I've already told you I'd let you know when y'all may go in the tunnel."

Mandie was tired and decided she might as well go to bed. Her friends agreed with the idea. It had been a long, tiring day.

She lay awake a long time, though, wondering what the crack looked like and whether the house could be in danger of caving in from the tunnel. It was a scary thought, and when she finally did go to sleep, she had a bad dream about it. She and her friends were in the tunnel inspecting the crack, when suddenly it popped wide open with a loud roar.

She gasped for breath and woke up to find Snowball curled up, purring in her ear. She pushed him away and pulled the cover over her head, wishing for the morning to come.

Chapter 3 / Unexpected Happenings

Mandie woke just as the sun peeped over the dark horizon. She decided to get up. Slipping quietly out of bed to keep from waking Celia, she quickly put on her clothes, picked up Snowball, who was sitting up on the bed washing his face, and quietly left the room, softly pulling the door to behind her.

As she walked softly down the hallway to the staircase, she didn't hear a sound. No one seemed to be up. She carried Snowball downstairs, went out the back hall door, and set him down in the yard. The white cat rubbed around her ankles and followed her as she walked around the house to the pathway down the hill.

"Now would be a good time to check the outside entrance to the tunnel," she said to herself.

She left the pathway and cut through the wooded part of the property. Snowball ran ahead of her as he found a squirrel to chase. Then suddenly the squirrel ran up a tree, and Snowball followed and stopped at the base of the tree. He looked back at Mandie and meowed.

"Don't you go up that tree," Mandie yelled at him. "I know you. Once you get up a tree, someone has to go up and get you down. You come here, you hear?"

Snowball sat still and looked at her. Mandie caught up with him, but when she reached down to pick him up, he quickly ran up the tree trunk and sat on the lower limb, out of her reach.

Mandie stomped her foot as she stood and looked up at him. "Snowball, I think I'll just leave you up there," she said.

Snowball looked down at her and meowed. Mandie moved directly under where he was sitting and tried to reach him, but the limb was too high. And Snowball just sat there and meowed.

"I think you are just going to have to stay there until Joe or Jonathan comes to get you down," Mandie said.

Suddenly a voice behind her said, "I get cat down, Papoose," and she turned to see Uncle Ned standing there. He smiled and quickly jumped up to catch the limb on which the cat was sitting. Holding on with one hand, the old man grabbed the white cat with his other hand. Snowball wriggled out of his grasp, landed on his four feet, and ran off into the woods, meowing like he was angry.

"Thank you, Uncle Ned," Mandie said as she watched the white fur disappear in the brush. She smiled and said, "I don't know why he has to run up trees and then can't seem to figure out how to get down."

"White cat knows how to get down, just playing tricks with Papoose," the old man said. "Next time leave him up there. When he gets hungry he will come down." He frowned and asked, "Why Papoose up so early?"

Mandie shuffled her feet in the underbrush and

replied, "I woke up early and thought I might as well get up and get some fresh air before breakfast." She paused to look up at the tall man and then added, "I had a bad dream last night."

"Dream about crack?" Uncle Ned asked.

"Yes, sir," Mandie replied, hugging her arms together. "It was roaring something awful, and I woke up to find Snowball purring in my ear." She shivered as she remembered the dream.

"We walk, Papoose," Uncle Ned said, leading the way on through the trees. He looked down at Mandie at his side and added, "Crack does not roar. Little size crack."

"Do you think the tornado caused the crack?" Mandie asked. The storm had not seemed to do any damage to the house at the time it went through.

"Yes, must have," Uncle Ned replied.

"What does the crack look like, Uncle Ned?" Mandie asked as they came out into the clearing.

Uncle Ned shrugged his shoulders and said, "Like crack."

Mandie smiled up at him and said, "What I meant was, is it a wide crack like this," and she held her two hands apart in front of her, then put them closer together and said, "Or like this?"

The old man frowned and said, "Like this," and he drew a crooked vertical line in the air in front of him.

Mandie smiled and said, "Then it's not a straight line of a crack, and it goes up and down and not crossways."

Uncle Ned bent, picked up a stick, and traced a crooked line in the dirt. "That way, that size," he said. He straightened up and added, "About six feet tall."

Mandie smiled at his description and said, "I understand. Can you see through the crack, Uncle Ned?"

He looked puzzled.

"Is the crack split open enough to see through it into whatever is behind it?" she added.

Uncle Ned nodded and said, "Dark behind crack."

"I suppose it would be, since that would be under the house," Mandie said. Then, looking up at the old man, she asked, "Do you have the key to the outside tunnel entrance? We're close to it; it's over there behind those trees." She pointed to their left.

"No key, Papoose. John Shaw keep key," he told her. Then glancing up at the sun in the sky, he added, "Time to go eat."

"Yes, sir," Mandie agreed, and they turned back toward the house. As they walked along, she thought to herself, *It wouldn't have done any good to go on to check the outside entrance to the tunnel. It would have been locked.*

When they got back to the kitchen, Aunt Lou, Jenny, the cook, and Liza were all there getting the morning meal ready.

Aunt Lou greeted them as they came in the back door. "Y'all jes' sit down right dere at de table. I bring coffee," she said.

"Oh, thank you, Aunt Lou," Mandie said as she and Uncle Ned sat where the old woman indicated.

Aunt Lou got two cups from the sideboard, took them to the huge iron cookstove, and picked up the percolator, steaming with coffee. She filled the cups and set them in front of Mandie and Uncle Ned. "Fresh made, good and strong," she said. "Git yo' minds to workin'."

The door opened, and Joe, Jonathan, and Celia came into the kitchen.

"Morning, everybody," Jonathan mumbled as though he were still half asleep.

Greetings were exchanged, and the three came to sit at the table with Mandie and Uncle Ned. Aunt Lou brought them cups of coffee.

"What time did you get up, Mandie? I didn't hear you," Celia said.

"About an hour ago, I think," Mandie said. "I woke up and decided to go out for a walk."

"Jonathan and I waited on the landing for you two, and then finally Celia came out of your room," Joe said. "Where have you been?" He looked directly at Mandie.

"Just for a walk in the woods with Snowball, and then he decided to chase a squirrel up a tree. Uncle Ned happened to come along, and he got him down for me," Mandie explained. She looked directly at him and added, "That's all." She knew he would understand that she had not been to the outside entrance of the tunnel as he had suspected.

"What are the plans for today?" Jonathan asked, sipping the hot coffee in his cup.

"Plans?" Mandie repeated. She looked at Uncle Ned and asked, "Do you know what plans Uncle John has for today?"

Uncle Ned shook his head and said, "Man come before noon sun to look at crack. Then we make plans."

"Plans to repair the crack," Jonathan said, nodding his head.

"Yes," Uncle Ned replied.

Mandie quickly looked at her friends and said, "Then we can go look at the crack this afternoon.

Uncle John said after the man inspected it he would let us go in and look."

"Yes," Jonathan said with a big grin.

"I'm not sure I want to go in that dark tunnel just to look at a crack," Celia said.

"But we always take lanterns with us. It won't be dark in there," Mandie assured her.

"Remember, Mandie, if your uncle thinks the crack is dangerous, he said he would not allow anyone in there," Joe reminded her.

"Well, we'll know about that when Uncle Ned's friend inspects it," Mandie replied.

Liza, listening to the conversation from the other side of the room, spoke up. "Lawsy mercy, Missy 'Manda, don't see why you wants to look at dat ol' crack. I ain't gwine down dere. Might crack wide open."

Everyone laughed.

"And it ain't no laughin' matter," Liza said quickly. "Dis heah house might be 'bout to fall in."

"Liza, you jes' hush dat crazy talk now, you heah?" Aunt Lou told the girl. "Git a move on now and git de dining room table set, right now."

"Yes'm," Liza said, going to the cupboard to get dishes.

By the time Aunt Lou got the food on the sideboard in the dining room, all the adults had come down, and everyone went in to eat. Mandie didn't dare ask Uncle John any more questions about the crack, but she listened to all the conversation at the table that she could hear. Not a word was said about the crack until the meal was finished and everyone stood up to go into the parlor for coffee.

Then she overheard John Shaw as he spoke to Uncle Ned. "Your friend should be here any minute now, shouldn't he?" he asked.

"Yes, any time now," Uncle Ned agreed.

Mandie whispered to her friends as they followed the adults into the parlor, "Did you hear that? The man will be here any time now."

All her friends nodded, and everyone found a seat in the parlor. Liza brought the coffee on the tea cart since there were so many people present. As soon as everyone had their coffee, there was a loud knock on the front door. Liza was still in the room, and she went to answer it.

Mandie heard her saying, "Dey all in de parlor."

Then Polly Cornwallis appeared in the doorway. "I thought I'd see what y'all are doing today," she said as she came on into the room and sat down on a chair near Joe.

"We have no idea as to what we'll be doing today, Polly," Mandie said, and she saw her mother glance at her from across the room.

Mrs. Taft, Mandie's grandmother, was sitting next to Senator Morton near Mandie's mother, Elizabeth. Mandie saw the two ladies speak to each other but couldn't hear what was said. Then Mrs. Taft spoke across the room. "Amanda, I thought we could go for a ride out into the countryside. The senator has never really seen the area around here."

Before Mandie could answer, Elizabeth said, "Oh yes, Amanda, you should go with Mother and take your friends along. The rest of us will be busy today."

"But, Mother, I'm not sure they want to go," Mandie replied.

Then Jonathan spoke up. "Yes, let's do go. I'd love to see the country." He looked at the other young people.

John Shaw was listening to the conversation, and he said, "Joe, if you would be good enough to drive the rig, I'd appreciate it. Abraham is going to be busy with other things today."

Joe grinned at Mandie, then looked at John Shaw and said, "Yes, sir, I'd be glad to drive the rig."

"Then I'll put everything in your hands," John Shaw said.

Mrs. Taft rose from her chair and said, "Then let's get started. I just need to go to my room for a few minutes and then I'll be ready."

Mandie finally figured out what was going on. Evidently her mother was trying to get Polly out of the house before the man came to inspect the crack in the tunnel. Everyone knew Polly was always telling everything she heard, and John Shaw had already cautioned the young people not to talk about the secret tunnel.

"Oh well," Mandie said as all her friends stood up. "Let me find Snowball so I can take him with us and I'll be ready." Turning to Polly, she asked, "Are you coming with us, Polly?"

Polly looked at everyone and asked, "How long will y'all be gone?"

Mrs. Taft was walking across the room, and she said, "A few hours, Polly. We're taking our noon meal with us. If you want to go, you are welcome."

"Well, I'll have to go ask my mother," Polly said.

"Then hurry," Mandie told her.

Polly rushed out of the room as Mrs. Taft went into the hallway to go to her room.

Mandie turned to her friends and said, "I'll be right back with Snowball." Then under her breath, she added, "This must have been planned beforehand."

All her friends smiled and nodded.

Joe drove the rig down the winding roads into the countryside. Mandie, with Snowball, sat beside him. Celia, Polly, and Jonathan were right behind them. Mrs. Taft and Senator Morton sat on the back-seat and carried on their own conversation.

Aunt Lou had quickly prepared a basket of food to send with them. Mandie knew they would be gone for a while and that the man coming to look at the crack would have been there and gone by the time they returned.

Even though Joe did not live near Franklin, he was familiar with the countryside because of having been with his father making his rounds many times. Mrs. Taft didn't give him any instructions, so he drove toward the mountain. And he knew who lived in practically every house they passed because, some time or other, most of the people had had to have his father doctor them.

"This is better than sitting around the house, isn't it?" Jonathan remarked, turning to the others.

"I suppose," Polly said.

"Yes," Celia said. "I knew the adults would be busy today, and I had been wondering what we would do."

"We could always have sat in the arbor or walked around town," Mandie said. Mrs. Taft and Senator Morton were not listening but were deep in a conversation of their own, in voices too low to understand over the rattle of the rig as they rode along.

After a long while, Mrs. Taft finally did speak up. "Joe, I believe we should stop to eat now whenever you find a suitable place," she said.

Joe glanced back and said, "Yes, ma'am. I know where there's a waterfall not far from here."

"Fine," Mrs. Taft said.

When Joe finally pulled the rig off the road beside a glistening waterfall, Snowball suddenly decided he wanted free. He managed to pull away from Mandie and jump down. Jonathan instantly went after him and barely caught his leash before he got away in the direction of the water.

"Please don't let that cat get away," Mrs. Taft told Mandie as everyone left the rig and the boys brought the basket of food to a rough log table with benches near the water.

"I won't," Mandie promised as she tied Snowball's leash to a bush near the water so he could drink from the pond.

As everyone sat around the table eating, Senator Morton said, "This is certainly beautiful country. I've never really been out this way before. I'm usually just in and out on the train."

"It's certainly different from your countryside in Florida," Mrs. Taft said as she ate a piece of fried chicken.

Mandie noticed that Aunt Lou had even put in linen napkins and a tablecloth, probably because it was for Mrs. Taft.

Turning to the young people, Mrs. Taft asked, "What do you all plan to do for the rest of your summer vacation?" She looked at Mandie.

Mandie instantly knew Mrs. Taft had something in mind for them to do. She quickly tried to think up an answer of some kind that would make her grandmother believe they already had plans, but she was not fast enough.

"My father and I will be going home as soon as he and Mr. Shaw get their little job done," Jonathan said.

"But that won't take long," Mrs. Taft said. "How would you all like to come visit with me back in Asheville? Hilda will be home, and it has been a while since y'all saw her."

Hilda was the girl Mandie and Celia had found living in the attic of their boarding school in Asheville, North Carolina. Mrs. Taft had taken the girl in to live with her. However, Hilda didn't talk and was hard to communicate with.

Celia glanced at Mandie. Mandie blew out her breath and said, "Grandmother, let us think about it."

Polly spoke up. "Am I invited, too, Mrs. Taft?"

Mrs. Taft looked at her and smiled as she said, "Of course, Polly, but you know you will have to ask your mother."

"Yes, ma'am, I will," Polly said. "She has been wanting to visit some friends over in Asheville, so maybe she could go, too. And we would all be back in Asheville to go back to school when it opens."

"Yes, your mother would be welcome, too, Polly," Mrs. Taft said.

Mandie turned her head to keep anyone from seeing her smile. Mrs. Taft had just become involved with Polly for the rest of the summer if they all agreed to go to her house. She couldn't imagine her grandmother being around Polly that long. Polly always seemed to get into messes of some kind every time she went anywhere with Mandie and her friends.

"My father will be coming for me any day," Joe said. "I want to go home and spend some time before I go back to college. And I plan to return in about two more weeks to take some special classes that I need to catch up with my class. But I thank you for asking me, Mrs. Taft."

"Just in case your plans are changed, Joe, you will be most welcome to come visit with the others," Mrs. Taft told him.

Mandie had already been thinking about what she should do with the rest of her summer vacation. All her friends seemed to have to go home, and she wasn't certain she wanted to go to her grandmother's house to stay before school opened. Maybe she would just stay home with her mother and Uncle John.

Mrs. Taft opened the lid on the little watch she wore on a chain around her neck and said, "Well, now, I believe we ought to be getting back. It's later than I thought."

Mandie and Celia quickly packed up what was left of the food into the basket. Joe put it in the rig.

"Shall I drive faster going back, Mrs. Taft? I mean, did we stay too long or something?" Joe asked as Senator Taft helped the lady back into the rig.

"Oh no, Joe, we're not late for anything that I know of," Mrs. Taft told him as she once again sat on the backseat with the senator.

Mandie held tightly to Snowball as her friends climbed back in and Joe drove out into the road.

"It was nice of you young people to take us out like this," Senator Morton said.

"Yes, I've enjoyed it, too," Mrs. Taft added.

"Grandmother, are you and all our parents planning anything for tonight?" Mandie asked as they rode along.

"Why no, Amanda, not that I know of. Now, your mother could have made some plans while we were gone," Mrs. Taft said.

Mandie was secretly hoping the grown-ups would be going out somewhere late that day because if Uncle John didn't let them go into the tunnel when they got back, she was going to figure out how to get her grandmother on her side to allow them in the tunnel. She just had to see that crack. And she hoped she would not dream about it again tonight.

Chapter 4 / Snowball Creates a Mystery

Whey they got back to the Shaws' house, there was no one home. Mandie went to the kitchen to ask Aunt Lou where everyone was. Polly went home.

"My chile, yo' mama and all dem other grown-ups dey done went off wid Miz Cornwallis in her rig," Aunt Lou explained.

"Did they say where they were going?" Mandie asked.

"No. Miz Lizbeth, she say dey be back in time fo' suppuh and to set four extry places," the old woman explained as she stirred a pot of green beans on the stove.

"Four extra places?" Mandie said. "I wonder who is going to have supper with us."

"I hears huh ask Miz Cornwallis to eat, and she say she will, she and dat daughter of hers," Aunt Lou replied. "But I don't be knowin' who de other people gwine be. Now, where yo' grandmother, chile, and dat senator? Do dey be wantin' coffee in de parlor?"

"Everybody is in the parlor that went with me, and I know they'd like coffee, Aunt Lou, especially if you have any of that chocolate cake left," Mandie said, smiling up at the woman.

"Oh, my chile, you gwine turn to chocolate one o' dese days," Aunt Lou replied with a big smile. "But I'se got plenty of dat cake in de cupboard. Jes' go tell Miz Taft de coffee and cake will be right in."

"Yes, ma'am, thank you," Mandie replied with a loving pat on Aunt Lou's shoulder.

Mrs. Taft and the senator were sitting on the far side of the parlor, and Mandie's friends were seated near the door. She went over to her grandmother.

"Everybody went off with Mrs. Cornwallis in her rig, and Aunt Lou said my mother told her to set places for four more people for supper tonight—Mrs. Cornwallis and Polly, and she didn't know who the other two would be. Do you?"

"Why, no, Amanda. I have no idea," Mrs. Taft said. "I hope you asked for coffee."

"Yes, ma'am, and chocolate cake," Mandie replied with a smile.

"I believe I could eat a piece of that cake this time," Senator Morton said.

Liza came in with the tea cart, and Mandie went over to sit with her friends. After Liza served Mrs. Taft and Senator Morton, she came over to the young people to pour their coffee and hand out the little plates of chocolate cake.

"Did the man come to look at the crack in the tunnel, Liza?" Jonathan asked as he set his coffee down on the end table by the settee.

"Oh, shucks!" Mandie suddenly said, blowing out her breath. "How could I forget to ask Aunt Lou about that? Did he come, Liza?"

"Some man come and went down in de tunnel wid all de men, but he didn't stay long, said he be in a hurry. And he got on his horse and hurried off down de road," the girl explained.

"Did you hear anything my uncle said about the crack in the tunnel?" Mandie asked.

"He jes' tell dat man we gotta fix it right quick 'fo' it falls in," Liza said. She danced around the room, hugging herself, and added, "I done told evy-body dis heah house might fall in."

"Did Uncle John say it was dangerous?" Mandie asked.

Liza stopped in front of Mandie and replied, "He say befo' dis heah house fall in. Don't dat mean dis heah house might be gwine fall in?"

"Maybe," Mandie said.

"Did you go down and look at the crack, Liza?" Jonathan asked, sipping his coffee.

"No siree, ain't gwine down in dat place, no I ain't," the girl replied. "I'se gotta go now 'fo' Aunt Lou come lookin' fo' me." She quickly left the par-lor.

Mandie looked at her friends and said, "I can't imagine who the other two people are for supper tonight, unless maybe one of them is the man who came to look at the crack."

"It might be," Celia agreed.

"I hope he does come back. Maybe we could hear what he says about the tunnel," Jonathan said.

"Liza said the man left in a hurry," Joe reminded them.

"I'd like to know exactly who he is, where he came from," Mandie said, sipping her coffee.

Joe hastily swallowed a mouthful of chocolate cake and said, "Remember, Mr. Shaw said the man was a friend of Uncle Ned's. He may be Cherokee."

"Yes," Mandie agreed, squishing the chocolate icing on her cake. "Anyhow, the adults are bound to discuss the man's visit tonight, and if we stay around them we can listen."

Mrs. Taft spoke from the other side of the parlor as she and the senator rose from their chairs. "Amanda, I am going to my room to rest for a little while, if your mother gets back and asks for me."

"And I am going to take a walk around the yard," Senator Morton said.

"Yes, ma'am, yes, sir," Mandie replied as the two left the room.

"Let's go sit in the kitchen," Jonathan suggested.

"Sit in the kitchen? Now, why do you want to do that?" Joe asked.

"Because I am not allowed to sit in our kitchen at home, and I love to talk to Aunt Lou," Jonathan explained with a big grin.

Mandie shrugged her shoulders and said, "Oh well, I suppose we could. Only I thought if we stayed in here we would know when my mother and the others return, and maybe they'll have those other two people with them who are coming to supper."

"Doesn't your mother always let Aunt Lou know when she returns from being out somewhere?" Celia asked.

Mandie nodded and said, "Most of the time." She rose. "Come on, let's go." She picked up her cake plate and coffee cup and saucer. "I might as well take these."

Her friends picked up their dishes.

"I'll just get those over there that Mrs. Taft and Senator Morton left, and we'll save Liza a trip from the kitchen," Joe said, going to the other side of the room and getting the dishes.

When the four young people opened the door

and entered the kitchen with all the dishes, Aunt Lou shook her head at them and said, "Now, whut fo' are y'all adoin' dat? We gits paid to do dat." She stepped forward to take some of the dishes and said to Liza, "Come heah and git dese heah dishes, Liza."

When the two had taken all the dishes from the young people, Jonathan asked with a big grin, "Aunt Lou, may we have permission to sit at your table for a little while?"

Aunt Lou reached to pat him on the shoulder as she crossed the room and said, "Since you be one of dem Yankee boys and don't know no better, I suppose it'd be all right for a few minutes, but mind you, we's busy in heah gittin' supper ready."

Jonathan, still grinning, replied, "Thank you, Aunt Lou, for the privilege."

"Oh, come on, Jonathan, and sit down," Mandie told him as she and the others pulled out chairs at the long table.

"Aunt Lou, did you see the man who came to look at the crack in the tunnel?" Mandie asked.

"I sho' did," Aunt Lou said, stirring several pots of food on the big iron cookstove. "He come right heah through my kitchen."

"What did he look like? Was he Cherokee? He's Uncle Ned's friend, you know," Mandie said.

"He sho' is Cherokee, and young and good-looking, too," the old woman replied, turning and wiping her hands on her large white apron.

"I wonder if I've ever met him, if he lives anywhere near Uncle Ned," Mandie said.

Aunt Lou shook her head and said, "Don't think so. He says he has to hurry back home to Asheville. And he was wearin' white man's clothes, not dressed like Uncle Ned."

Mandie frowned as she and her friends looked at each other. "Asheville," she said. "I wonder if he has ever been around our school there."

"Probably not, Mandie," Celia said. "I don't remember ever seeing any Cherokee workmen around there."

"He's comin' back," Aunt Lou told her as she turned once again to stir the contents of the pots on the stove. "I hears him say he's comin' back."

"When is he coming back?" Mandie asked.

"I don't know, my chile. He went out de door about dat time," Aunt Lou replied. "Now, where dat Polly girl whut went wid y'all this afternoon?"

"She went home as soon as we got back," Mandie told her. "She said she was tired and dirty." She grinned at the thought.

"Well, I s'pects she'll be back tonight wid her mama," Aunt Lou said.

Liza was peeling potatoes at the sideboard and listening to the conversation. "She sho' will, wid two boys heah now," she said with a big grin.

Everyone laughed.

"Maybe the other two people expected for supper will be girls," Jonathan said, grinning at the others.

"That would make things interesting," Joe agreed, glancing at Mandie with a mischievous smile.

"Or they could be boys," Mandie said, grinning back.

"Or they could be older people," Celia added.

Aunt Lou was listening to their conversation. "Y'all jes' seem bound and determined to decide who's coming to eat tonight, but I thinks y'all just gwine hafta wait and see." She smiled at them.

Mandie instantly had the idea that Aunt Lou knew but didn't want to tell them who was expected. "Aunt Lou, why don't you tell us who is coming?" she asked with a big smile.

"Now, my chile, I ain't said I knows," Aunt Lou replied. "Now why don't y'all git out of my kitchen so I kin git supper ready? Shoo now."

Mandie and her friends laughed as they stood up.

"Yes, ma'am," Mandie said with a big grin. "We'll just go outside and find the senator and see what he is doing."

"Yes," Joe agreed. "He went out alone."

"Come on, then," Jonathan said, starting for the door.

Celia caught up with Mandie as they stepped into the hallway. "Mandie, I'll need to change clothes for supper," she said. "I feel dirty after that trip into the country."

"Yes, and I'll have to change, too," Mandie agreed. "But we have plenty of time for that."

The four went out the back door and looked around the yard, but there was no sign of Senator Morton.

"Maybe he came back inside and went to his room," Joe suggested.

"Let's walk down to the outside entrance to the tunnel," Mandie said, leading the way without looking to see whether her friends were following or not.

"It won't be unlocked," Joe reminded her as he followed.

Celia and Jonathan straggled behind.

When Mandie got to the outside entrance, hidden by vines, bushes, and trees, she was surprised to find Senator Morton sitting on a log nearby. He looked up as she approached.

"Is the door unlocked, Senator Morton?" Mandie asked, hurrying to investigate. The door was closed.

"No. I thought perhaps it would be, but no, it's locked," the senator replied. "So I thought I'd just sit here awhile and watch the birds and the squirrels. Your white cat has been chasing them." He smiled at her.

Mandie quickly looked around and saw Snowball crouched in the bushes, intently watching something hidden from her view. Her friends caught up with her.

"Oh, shucks, I was hoping the door would be unlocked," Mandie said, blowing out her breath.

"Yes, I thought the men might have left it open," Senator Morton said. "I wanted to have a look at the crack and see what could be done to repair it since I offered to help."

"Aunt Lou said the man was coming back, but she didn't know when," Mandie told him. "And she also said we are having two unidentified guests at supper tonight. Maybe one will be that man."

The four young people sat down on a nearby log.

"Have y'all decided to go home with Mrs. Taft for a visit?" the senator asked.

"No, sir, I haven't decided," Mandie said, glancing at her friends.

They all shook their heads.

"I have to wait and see what my mother wants to do," Celia said.

Suddenly Snowball quickly backed out of the bushes where he had been sitting. He growled and hit at something he was pulling along with his paw.

Mandie leaned forward to see what the cat was doing. "Snowball, what have you got there?" she asked.

The cat continued batting at something in the

grass. Mandie got up to look. "Snowball, where did you get that?" she asked in surprise. He had a red velvet pincushion with several pins in it. She took it from him and examined it.

"A pincushion?" Celia said.

"Now, what would a cat want with a pincushion?" Jonathan teased as he watched Mandie turning it over in her hand.

"Maybe that cat has learned to sew," Joe added with a big grin.

Mandie was puzzled. "Yes, it is a pincushion, but where did it come from?" she said.

Snowball reached up to get his toy back from her as he meowed loudly.

"No, Snowball, you cannot have this back. In the first place, it has pins in it, and besides, it doesn't look dirty, so someone must have dropped it here recently." She turned it over and held it up for her friends to see.

"Aha, we have another mystery to solve," Jonathan said, grinning at her as he looked at the pincushion.

"Senator Morton, has Snowball been there in that bush the whole time you've been here?" Mandie asked.

"I believe so," he replied. "I remember seeing him through the bushes and wondering what he was doing down here without you."

"He does wander off without me when we're at home, like now," Mandie explained. "This morning he ran up a tree over there, and Uncle Ned happened to come by and got him down for me. But I would like to know where this pincushion came from. It's not dirty, and it doesn't look like it's been out here long."

"It doesn't look familiar to me," Celia said. "I don't believe I have seen it in your house."

"It doesn't belong to me," Mandie said. She bent over to fan the bushes aside where Snowball had found the pincushion. "I don't see anything else around here."

"Maybe someone in the house will recognize it," Joe suggested.

"But I can't imagine how a pincushion got down here," Mandie said.

"Maybe Snowball got it somewhere in the house and brought it down here," Jonathan said.

Mandie shook her head. "No, I imagine someone in the house would have seen him with it and taken it away. He must have just found it right here in the bushes."

"Do you know who it could possibly belong to?" Jonathan asked.

"No," Mandie replied. "I'll ask Liza if she has seen it before."

"Mandie, remember we have to clean up for supper, and it must be getting late," Celia reminded her.

"Yes, let's go back to the house," Mandie agreed. Looking down at her white cat, she said, "Come on, Snowball, let's go." She held the pincushion down just out of his reach, and he went with her up the path.

Senator Morton and the other young people followed Mandie back into the house.

"I shall see you all at supper. I must also get freshened up," the senator told them as he went on toward the staircase, and Mandie and her friends went to open the kitchen door.

Snowball darted ahead of everyone as soon as the door was opened.

Aunt Lou called to them from the stove, where she was still stirring pots of food. "Now, I done tol' y'all to git out 'cause I gotta git de supper done."

"We are not staying," Mandie replied as she held up the pincushion. "I only want to show you this and ask if you've seen it before."

Liza was getting dishes down from the cupboard. She turned to look. "I ain't seen it before," she said as she glanced at the pincushion.

"No, I don't believe I have, either," Aunt Lou said. "What are you adoin' totin' a pincushion around?"

Mandie explained where she had found it. "I thought maybe y'all might know where it came from," she added.

"Skiddoo," Aunt Lou said. "Y'all has to git outta heah so I can finish gittin' de supper ready now."

"All right, all right, we're going," Mandie quickly replied and followed her friends out into the hallway. Then she remembered her mother and the others who had gone off somewhere that day. Stopping to step back and push the door open, she asked, "Do y'all know if my mother and the others have come back yet?"

"Ain't seen 'em. Now git goin', my chile, 'fo' I burns up de supper," Aunt Lou told her.

Mandie quickly stepped back into the hallway and followed her friends to the main staircase, where they all paused for a few minutes.

"Let's meet back here in twenty minutes," Mandie told her friends.

They all agreed and everyone went on to their rooms.

Mandie laid the pincushion on her bureau. "I'm going to leave this here, but I'm also going to ask my mother and grandmother whether they are missing a pincushion," she said as she went over to the wardrobe to take down a dress.

"It probably does belong to someone in your house here," Celia agreed, reaching for a fresh dress, also. "Things are getting complicated. Now we have two mysteries, the crack and the pincushion."

"Actually we have three mysteries unsolved, those two and the identity of who is coming to supper tonight," Mandie reminded her. She quickly removed her dress and slipped into the fresh one.

"At least we ought to be able to solve that one when everyone goes in to supper," Celia said, buttoning up the front of her new dress.

"Maybe we will find out before if we hurry and go down and wait in the parlor," Mandie said. "That is, if whoever it is comes back with my mother and the others."

The girls hurried and were back on the steps before the boys.

Chapter 5 / One Mystery Solved

"Let's go sit in the parlor," Mandie told her friends at the staircase. "My mother and the others have to come home before supper, and maybe they will have the two extra guests with them."

As they walked down the hallway, Joe asked, "Suppose these two extra people are ones you don't like?"

Mandie paused to look up at him and ask, "Someone I don't like? I don't believe my mother would invite someone like that."

"You never know. It might be for business purposes," Jonathan reminded her as he, too, stopped in the hallway.

"If y'all aren't coming to the parlor, I am. I want to sit down and relax for a while," Celia told the others. She continued toward the parlor door. The others followed.

As soon as they sat down in the parlor, Mandie looked across the room at the doorway and saw Snowball rush in carrying the red pincushion. She jumped up to take it away from him.

"Snowball, how did you get that pincushion back so fast?" she said to him as he protested losing the pincushion to her.

"He must have followed us up to your room, Mandie," Celia said.

Mandie sat down, holding the pincushion as she turned it over and over. "Probably," she agreed. "I don't really remember where he went when we got back to the house."

"What are you going to do with that thing?" Jonathan asked.

"I want to find out where it came from," Mandie replied. "And who it belongs to."

"That may be hard to do since you found it all the way down by the outside entrance to the tunnel," Joe reminded her.

Mandie grinned at him and said, "Don't you understand? If I can find out who this belongs to, then I will know who was poking around the tunnel entrance."

"And what good will that do you?" Jonathan asked.

"Jonathan, I just don't like things to be unexplained," Mandie said. "Whoever dropped this pincushion down there was on our property and may have been trying to get into the tunnel. And I would like to know why."

Mrs. Taft and Senator Morton came into the parlor and looked around as they took seats across the room from the young people.

"I suppose your mother and the others are not back yet, Amanda," Mrs. Taft said.

"No, ma'am, we've been waiting in here for them," Mandie replied. She held up the red pincushion as she got up and walked over to her grandmother's chair. "Have you ever seen this red pincushion before, Grandmother?"

Mrs. Taft looked puzzled as she glanced at the

pincushion and then at Mandie. "Why, no, I don't believe I have. Is there something wrong with it?"

"No, ma'am," Mandie replied. "Snowball was playing with it at the outside entrance to the tunnel when we walked down there, and I was wondering where it came from."

"Snowball was playing with a pincushion? It's a wonder he didn't get injured on it," Mrs. Taft said, frowning as she looked at the red object.

"Yes, ma'am, but I suppose I caught him in time," Mandie agreed. She had started back across the room to her chair when someone knocked on the front door. She immediately went out into the hallway to answer it.

When Mandie opened the front door, Polly was standing there. "Well, come on in, Polly," she said to the girl.

Polly fluffed her full skirt with one hand as she followed Mandie into the parlor. She immediately sat down in an empty chair next to Joe.

"My mother hasn't returned yet, so I thought I'd just come on over and wait since she and I will be having supper with y'all," Polly said to Mandie.

"Surely they will be back any time now. It's almost suppertime," Mandie said.

"Do you know yet how much longer you will be here, Joe?" Polly asked.

"I'm waiting for my father so I don't know exactly," Joe replied, straightening up in his chair as Polly leaned over.

Polly looked across at Jonathan and asked him, "How about you, Jonathan? Will you be staying here awhile yet?"

Jonathan shrugged his shoulders and said, "I have no idea. It all depends on my father."

"It must be nice to have a father to make all those decisions for y'all," Polly said. "I haven't had a father since I was a baby. In fact, I'm not even sure I can remember him. I always wanted my mother to get married again after my father died, but she has no plans for that."

"You ought to be glad your mother hasn't re-married, because she might marry someone you don't like," Jonathan told her.

Mandie was turning the pincushion over and over in her hands as she listened, and then she became aware of Polly watching her.

"What are you doing with that pincushion, Mandie?" Polly asked.

"Nothing, really," Mandie replied. "I found it. Snowball was playing with it."

"He was?" Polly asked in surprise. "Where did Snowball get it?"

"Down by the outside entrance to the tunnel," Mandie said.

"Oh, have y'all been in the tunnel?" Polly asked, looking around at the four young people.

As everyone shook their heads, Mandie said, "No, it's locked and we don't have the key."

"Where is the key?" Polly asked. "Why don't y'all have it?"

Mandie became exasperated with the questions. "We don't have the key because Uncle John has it," she said, frowning at the girl.

There was another knock on the front door, and Mandie heard Liza, who was evidently in the hall, open it. She couldn't hear what was being said.

Then everyone looked up to see Dr. and Mrs. Woodard standing in the doorway of the parlor.

"Dad! Mother!" Joe said in surprise as he stood

up. "I'm glad you came so I can go back home before returning to school."

Mrs. Taft had also stood up, and she said, "Welcome. Elizabeth and all the others are out somewhere, so come on in and make yourselves at home."

Mrs. Woodard went over to sit by Mrs. Taft and Senator Morton. Dr. Woodard pulled an envelope out of his inside coat pocket and handed it to Joe. "You have a letter here from your college," he said as he sat down.

Joe took it and quickly tore it open. He scanned the one page and looked up at his father with a big grin. "I don't have to go back to college early. They have scheduled the extra classes I need to catch up during the afternoons, when we normally have breaks."

"That's wonderful, son," Dr. Woodard said, smiling.

"Yes, Joe, I'm so glad your vacation won't be cut short," his mother said across the room.

Joe looked around at his friends. "What a relief! Now I can have a whole vacation," he told them.

"Then you should all come home with me and spend at least a few days," Mrs. Taft said across the room.

The young people all looked at each other and didn't reply. Mandie said, "Grandmother, we'll discuss it and let you know what our plans are now that Joe is free for the summer."

"All right, Amanda, but you are all welcome at my house," Mrs. Taft replied.

Mrs. Woodard spoke up. "You could all just come home with us and visit for a while," she said, then turned to Mrs. Taft and added, "And of course that includes you and Senator Morton."

Mandie laughed and said, "Since people want us all to go different places, it might be better if we all just stayed here at my house for the rest of the summer."

"We'll see, Amanda," Mrs. Taft said.

"Yes, we can decide later after we talk to your mother, Amanda," Mrs. Woodard said.

Then Mandie heard the front door open and close and all the other adults came into the room— her mother; Uncle John; Jonathan's father; Uncle Ned; Polly's mother, Mrs. Cornwallis; Celia's mother, Jane Hamilton; and John Shaw's caretaker, Jason Bond.

As greetings were being exchanged, Liza came to the doorway and announced loudly, "Miz Lizbeth, suppah be ready."

Elizabeth turned and said, "Thank you, Liza. Please ask Aunt Lou to give us about fifteen minutes to freshen up, and we'll be in."

"Yes'm," Liza replied and disappeared down the hallway.

Elizabeth said, "I need to clean up a little. How about y'all?"

All the people who had been with her agreed and immediately left the room, with a promise to return in fifteen minutes.

Mandie sighed and said, "Oh, shucks, we won't have time to talk to any of them before we eat."

Then suddenly Jonathan spoke up. "Now we know who the two other guests are, Joe's parents." He grinned at Mandie.

"Yes," Mandie and her friends all agreed.

"And I'm glad it was them, because they brought me good news," Joe said.

As soon as everyone returned to the parlor, Elizabeth Shaw led the way to the dining room. Mandie was pleased to notice that because of the many adults present, the seating allowed the young people to sit closer to them and, therefore, to hear at least part of their conversation.

Mandie was still carrying the pincushion, and not knowing what else to do with it, she placed it on the table by her plate. Elizabeth Shaw noticed this and spoke from the other end of the table. "Why, Amanda, what are you doing with a pincushion at the table?"

Mandie frowned and reached to pick it up. "I just had it in my hand and forgot to leave it in the parlor while we eat," she explained.

"Where did you get it in the first place?" Elizabeth asked.

All the adults had turned to look at the pincushion.

"I found it," Mandie replied.

Mrs. Cornwallis spoke up. "That looks like one that belongs to Polly." And glancing toward her daughter, she asked, "Is it yours, Polly?"

Polly stuttered with her answer, looking at the pincushion as she spoke. "Ah, no, ma'am, uh, that is, I don't think so."

The adults turned their attention to their own conversation. But Mandie had immediately noticed Polly's discomfort with the question from her mother. "It does belong to you, doesn't it, Polly?" she asked, holding it out to the girl across the table.

Polly took it, shook her head, and said, "I—I don't—uh—really know." She laid it down on the table.

"And you lost it at the outside entrance to our

tunnel," Mandie said, low enough that the adults could not hear her. "What were you doing down there, Polly?"

Polly frowned, bit her lip, and said, "What do you mean, what was I doing down there? I didn't say I had been down there."

"We'll talk about it later," Mandie told her. She planned to get Polly away from the adults and ask her some questions.

Polly shrugged her shoulders and began eating.

Mandie was determined she was going to find out what the girl had been doing, but she heard her uncle mention the tunnel and she quit talking to listen.

"Uncle Ned's friend will return the first thing tomorrow morning, and we can go to work on that crack then," John Shaw was saying to the other adults.

"And according to him it shouldn't take more than a day to repair it," Lindall Guyer added.

Senator Morton laid down his fork and said, "I'm sorry I missed out on the plans, but I would like to help in any way I can."

"Thank you, Senator," John Shaw said. "Cliff, Uncle Ned's friend, examined the place and thought we could just add mortar to close it up and that it would be all right. In other words, he didn't seem to think it was dangerous."

"I see," Senator Morton replied. "Is this a crack with empty space behind it, or is it up against a wall?"

"We couldn't really tell, but we assumed the stairway where it's located was dug out just for the steps," John Shaw replied. "Therefore it would be solid dirt behind it."

"I would suggest you make sure of that," Senator Morton told him. "If there is a hollow space behind it, the crack could reopen after a while."

"I thought when we start work on it we could open a place in it just enough to see what's behind it," John Shaw replied.

"That's an intelligent decision," the senator agreed.

The young people were all listening to the conversation.

Suddenly Mandie remembered her uncle telling them to keep this problem secret, just within the family, and here he was talking about it in front of Mrs. Cornwallis and Polly and also Dr. and Mrs. Woodard. The Woodards were like kinpeople, but the Cornwallises were not. Polly loved to tote tales of anything she heard.

"Maybe they will allow us to look at the crack when they start to repair it," Jonathan said, looking around at the young people.

"Yes, I would like to see that crack," Polly spoke up.

"You would?" Mandie asked, watching her closely.

"Yes, wouldn't you?" Polly replied. "I heard your cook telling our cook about it yesterday, and I told my mother."

"You did?" Mandie said.

"Yes, and she said she didn't care to go down in that tunnel and look at it, but I would," Polly explained.

Mandie sighed and looked at her friends.

"Maybe we can all go down there together and look," Joe suggested.

"We will have to ask Uncle John," Mandie reminded him.

"Yes, of course," Joe agreed.

"If they get the crack repaired tomorrow, does that mean you and your father will be leaving the next day, Jonathan?" Mandie asked.

"I'll have to speak to him and find out," Jonathan replied.

As soon as the meal was over, everyone returned to the parlor for coffee. Mandie and her friends followed, hoping to hear more conversation regarding the crack in the tunnel. However, the adults were talking mainly about the friends they had been to visit that day.

After a while, Liza came to the parlor doorway and held up the red pincushion. "Somebody forgit dis heah thang?" she asked as she looked around at the young people.

Mandie waited for Polly to claim it, but she just looked at Liza and didn't say a word.

"I think it belongs to Polly," Mandie said.

Liza stepped inside the room and dropped it on the table next to where Polly was sitting. Then she turned and left the parlor.

When Polly didn't pick it up, Mandie said, "Take it, Polly; it must be yours."

Polly looked at it and finally picked it up as she said, "I'm not sure it's mine." She turned it over and over.

"You can take it home with you and see if yours is missing," Mandie said. She was positive it did belong to Polly, but she couldn't figure out how it came to be at the entrance of the tunnel.

"What are you girls planning on doing after you graduate next summer?" Jonathan asked.

"I'm not sure," Mandie told him. "Grandmother never has said whether she will give us all a trip to Europe for graduation or not. I imagine she will, but she will probably wait until the last minute to let us know. You know how she is about wanting to run everything, and she would want this to look like she had come up with the idea of a European trip herself." Mandie smiled at her friends.

"Are you going home with her for a visit before your school opens?" Joe asked.

"No, I don't think I want to," Mandie said. "What would we do for the rest of the summer at her house in Asheville?"

"Oh, you always find a mystery wherever you go," Jonathan told her with a big grin.

"Do you think your father might allow you to stay here for a while after he goes home?" Mandie asked.

"I'm not sure what he is planning. I know he has to go back to work, so he won't be home to do anything," Jonathan replied. Then in a whisper he added, "I thought maybe your grandmother and my father might become friends again."

Mandie smiled and said, "I thought so, too. However, the senator is here, and he takes up all her time. Maybe if the senator had not come, it would have happened."

Polly overheard the conversation, and she quickly asked, "Do y'all mean Mrs. Taft and Mr. Guyer don't like each other or something?"

"Oh goodness," Mandie said.

"They are not exactly close friends," Jonathan said.

"Did they have a quarrel or something?" Polly asked.

"Oh, Polly, they used to be friends when they were young," Mandie said. "Does your mother have any men friends from long ago like that?"

Polly thought for a moment and said, "She has had lots of men friends over the years I've been growing up, but I don't think there was any special one."

Mandie was relieved to see Mrs. Cornwallis rise and announce, "I believe we had better be getting back home now. We greatly enjoyed your company today." Looking across the room, she said, "Polly, we must go now."

Polly stood up and said, "Yes, ma'am."

Mandie blew out her breath in relief. Polly was not going to ask to stay longer.

After Polly and her mother had departed, Mandie said, "I just know that pincushion must belong to Polly, but I can't figure out how it happened to get to the entrance of our tunnel."

"I agree that it must be hers, but I have no idea as to why she would be carrying a pincushion around with her," Celia said.

"We may never know," Joe said.

"She is a strange girl, so there was probably some strange reason why she had it down there by the tunnel entrance," Jonathan said.

"She was probably snooping to see if the tunnel was locked after she heard about the crack, but I don't think she would go inside the tunnel by herself, and besides, what would a pincushion have to do with it, anyway?" Mandie said.

———

After Mandie went to bed that night she thought about Polly and the pincushion for a long time but never could get the slightest idea of what the girl was doing with it.

She also thought about the crack in the tunnel and wondered if her uncle would allow them inside to look at it before the men covered it up. She intended being up early the next morning before the man arrived. Maybe if she asked Uncle John, he would allow her and her friends to go inside.

And then there was another thing that she thought about. Although her grandmother and Jonathan's father had seemed to forget their differences and become friends again while they were visiting Jonathan's house, the two didn't seem to ever even speak to each other now. Had something else happened to cause a break in their friendship?

So many problems to solve.

Chapter 6 / The Intruder

Mandie quietly slipped out of bed the next morning, trying not to wake Celia, but Celia awoke anyway.

"Is it time to get up?" Celia asked as Mandie put on her dress.

Mandie turned to look at her. "It's early, but I wanted to get downstairs before the man comes to repair the crack," she told Celia. "Maybe Uncle John will allow us to go in the tunnel with him."

"Oh yes," Celia said, quickly getting out of bed, upsetting Snowball, who was curled up at the foot. He rose, stretched, and began washing his face.

The girls weren't the first to come down to the kitchen. John Shaw, Jonathan, and Joe were sitting at the table, drinking coffee.

"Good afternoon," Jonathan teased the girls when they came into the room.

"Y'all must have stayed up all night," Mandie replied. She and Celia went to the stove to fill cups of coffee and bring them to the table, where they sat down.

"Not all night, just half of it," Joe said, grinning at the girls as he sipped his coffee.

"The coffee tastes like you made it, Uncle John," Mandie said, drinking from her cup. "Good."

John Shaw smiled at her and said, "Don't let Aunt Lou hear you say that. She might refuse to ever make any more coffee for us."

"Is anyone else up?" Celia asked.

"Yes, Uncle Ned and Lindall have gone for a walk," John Shaw replied. He looked across the room at the door, which was being opened. "And here is Senator Morton. Good morning, sir. Come join us for a cup of coffee."

Mandie jumped up to get another cup. "Sit down, Senator Morton; I'll get your coffee," she said, filling the cup and bringing it to the table.

"I thought I'd better come on down and see if the man had arrived for the repairs," Senator Morton said, sitting down and picking up the cup of coffee. Turning to Mandie, he added, "Thank you, ma'am."

"Not yet, but he should be here shortly. Uncle Ned and Lindall are outside and will let us know when he arrives," John Shaw explained.

Mandie sat down at the side of the table next to her friends, and they listened to the conversation between her uncle and the senator.

"Will this man, Cliff, be able to do the job alone, or will he need some help?" Senator Morton asked.

"He seemed to think he could do it all," John Shaw said. "He's bringing his own supplies and equipment."

Senator Morton cleared his throat and then asked, "Do you think it would be possible for me to see this crack before the man gets the place tied up?"

"Oh yes, of course, I'm sorry, sir," John Shaw replied. "I didn't realize you were interested in seeing the place." He turned to look at Joe and said, "Joe, do you think you could get some lanterns and take the senator down to see the damage? I need to stay here and watch for the repairman."

"Yes, sir," Joe replied with a big grin as he quickly stood up.

Mandie also rose as she asked, "Uncle John, could—"

"Yes," John Shaw quickly interrupted her. "You may all go look, but mind you, don't stay too long." He handed Joe the key, which he had had in his pocket.

All the young people had started to rush out of the kitchen when Mandie stopped, looked back, and asked, "Uncle John, whereabouts is this crack? How far up in the tunnel is it? How do we find it?"

John Shaw laughed and replied, "Yes, I suppose I'd better give you some idea as to where to look. The crack is under the house, so you'll need to go all the way up from the outside entrance to the last set of steps, which go under the foundation of the house. Understand?"

Mandie nodded. She had been in the tunnel many times and knew the pathway it took.

"It's in the wall on the right just as you get to those last steps, and it extends from the step several feet up," John Shaw explained.

"Yes, sir, I understand. I can find it," Mandie replied, turning to rush on out with her friends.

"Remember, just go look and come right back," John Shaw reminded them. "The repairman will be here anytime now, and you should all be out of his way."

Senator Morton stood up and said, "I suppose I'd better get along, too, and follow them." He smiled as he hurried after the young people.

Joe knew where the lanterns were kept in the closet in the hallway by the back door. He opened the door and stepped inside.

Mandie and her other friends stood watching and waiting as Joe handed a lantern to Mandie and reached for the matches on a shelf.

"How about giving me a lantern, too?" Jonathan asked. "Just in case one goes out."

"Yes, the more lanterns the better," Celia said. "I know how dark it can get in there without a lantern, like the time Mandie and I lost the matches and the lantern went out."

Senator Morton, standing by and waiting, said, "Perhaps you, too, should take one."

"Yes, sir," Joe agreed and took a lantern for himself. He looked around and said, "All right, we have three lanterns between us. That ought to be enough." He stepped back into the hallway and closed the closet door.

As the group left the house and started down the hill, Senator Morton said, "You know, this is quite an adventure for me. I've never been in the tunnel."

Mandie, walking along by his side, said, "It's good the door wasn't unlocked when you were down here before, because if you had gone in there without a lantern, you wouldn't have been able to see your way back out, Senator Morton."

"Yes, I realize that now," the senator agreed. "But then, if I had taken a few steps inside and seen how dark it was, I probably wouldn't have gone any farther."

"Do you know the history of the tunnel?" Mandie asked, looking up at the tall man as the group hurried on down the hill.

"Yes, I believe I have heard enough bits and pieces to put it all together," Senator Morton replied. "John Shaw's grandfather, who was your great-grandfather, built the tunnel to hide his Cherokee friends from the white soldiers who were forcing all the Indian people to leave the country around here during the Removal in 1838."

"Yes, sir," Mandie agreed, smiling up at him. "And my grandmother was full-blooded Cherokee. That's Uncle John's mother."

Joe was walking ahead. He paused to look back and asked, "Am I walking too fast? Mr. Shaw said we should hurry."

Everyone else hurried to catch up with him.

"Not too fast for me," Senator Morton said. "He's right. We should get this over with so we are not in the way of the workman."

Everyone was silent as they neared the entrance to the tunnel. Mandie quickly looked around the area. She thought she had heard a rustle and also believed she saw a flash of something moving into the trees and bushes. The entrance to the tunnel was kept overgrown with such in order to hide it from anyone passing through. Although it was on John Shaw's property, sometimes other people cut through the area and came out on the main road a few hundred yards ahead.

"Oh well," she said to herself, "I don't have time to investigate." She moved up with Joe as he unlocked the door and pushed it open.

"Senator, since you have not been in here before, I should warn you," Joe explained. "The corridor is very rough and uneven, and there are lots of steps now and then." He passed out matches, and

Mandie and Jonathan lit their lanterns as he also put a match to his.

"Thank you for the warning, Joe," Senator Morton replied.

"Why don't you walk along with me?" Jonathan said. "I have a lantern to light the way."

"Yes, that is a good idea. Thanks," the senator said, stepping inside behind Mandie and Celia, who were staying close to Joe. He looked around the interior. "Yes, this is quite a dark place and very interesting, the way it was cut out under the hill."

"One day when we have time I'll take you down into this tunnel from the other end. There is a secret door in Uncle John's office," Mandie told him, glancing back as she held her long skirts up with one hand and carried the lantern in the other.

As they made their way up the rough steps, Mandie thought about the something or someone she had heard outside at the entrance. Then she remembered that Uncle John had said Mr. Guyer and Uncle Ned were out walking somewhere. It was probably them going through the woods. But on the other hand, why didn't they stop to wave or speak to them? No, maybe it wasn't them. But who?

Joe slowed down as he began searching for the place where John Shaw had said the crack was. Mandie flashed her lantern up and down the walls. John Shaw had said it was in the wall on the right.

"Here it is," Joe said, a few steps ahead of her. "Look." He flashed his lantern on a large crack in the cement wall. Everyone crowded close to look. The crack was wide at the steps and narrowed off up the wall.

"That is a serious crack, I'd say," Senator Morton said, bending to run his hand down part of it.

Mandie quickly looked at the senator and asked, "Do you mean it could be dangerous?"

"No, not exactly, that is if it is repaired right away," the senator explained. "It's serious due to the fact that it is open and will take a lot of mortar to close it up. However, I don't think the house is in any danger."

Mandie got closer, flashed her lantern on it, and tried to see through the crack. The others crowded behind her.

"It's not wide enough to see through," Joe remarked.

Mandie tried to poke her finger through, but the crack was not wide enough. Her finger almost got stuck.

"Miss Amanda, I don't believe I'd do that," the senator warned her as he watched. "If your finger got stuck, we'd have to break part of the wall open to get it out."

"Yes, sir," Mandie said, quickly rubbing her finger down the back of her dress. The edges of the crack had slightly scratched it.

"How would you go about repairing this, Senator?" Joe asked.

Senator Morton cleared his throat and said, "First of all, you will have to remove any loose pieces of mortar, then press new mortar as far through the crack as you can and, of course, add more to smooth it off on the outside here. It is not a really big job. It will just take time. The first mortar should be allowed to dry a little before adding more, so that it will be firm through and through."

"You don't think the house is in danger, then," Mandie said.

"I would say it isn't. Look at all the other walls

here that are holding up the house," Senator Morton replied.

"Do you think it was caused by the tornado we had in the spring?" Mandie asked.

"Possibly," the senator answered. "As old as this tunnel is, probably from the year 1838, since there evidently hasn't been any damage to it before in the sixty-something years since it was built, I'd say it was the result of the tornado."

"I wonder if your uncle has inspected the whole tunnel and foundation of the house," Jonathan said to Mandie as he listened.

"Jonathan, that's scary," Mandie said. "If it was the tornado and it did this much damage, it could have done something else under here." She quickly looked around.

Senator Morton spoke up. "Don't worry about it. I'm sure your uncle has made a thorough inspection of the whole area."

"I hope so," Celia muttered as she wrapped her arms around herself and glanced around in the faint rays of light from the lantern in the underground depths.

Mandie held her lantern up close to the crack in an effort to see through it. She squinted and leaned over to look. "I just wish I could see what's behind this crack," she said.

"When the workman removes the loose mortar, you might be able to see through the crack," Senator Morton said.

"Do you mean he has to make the crack bigger in order to repair it?" Mandie asked in surprise.

"Not exactly," Senator Morton explained. "If there is any loose mortar along the edges of the crack, he may have to remove it, but that wouldn't be enough to open up the crack."

"I wish I could watch him do the work," Mandie said.

"I think we'd better be getting back now," Joe said. "Mr. Shaw told us not to stay too long."

"Yes, you are right," Senator Morton agreed as he turned to go back down the passageway.

Joe led the way ahead of the senator in order to light up the steps as they went.

Mandie, coming along with her lantern, asked, "Do y'all think Uncle John might allow us to watch from a distance as the man does the repair work?"

Joe glanced back at her as they all descended the steps in the tunnel and said, "No, Mandie, I'm sure he won't."

"Well, it wouldn't hurt to ask," Mandie said.

"Oh, Mandie, what if the wall decided to cave in when the man starts clearing the crack to repair it?" Celia asked.

"You think up the worst things sometimes, Celia," Mandie told her.

Senator Morton spoke up. "There is a possibility of a little of the wall falling when he begins on it, but it's not very likely if he knows how to do the job correctly."

"And he must know, because Uncle Ned recommended him," Mandie said, flashing her lantern along the way as they continued.

"As far as watching the man do the repair, one other problem would be that the space is not large enough to hold other people," Senator Morton reminded her. "The repairman has to have space enough to work."

"But I could stay a few steps down from the crack and look up and watch him," Mandie said.

"Your uncle is not going to agree to that, and you know it, Mandie," Joe said.

"I see the outside door ahead. Let's hurry and get out of here," Celia told the others.

"Don't get in too big a hurry. You could fall down these steps. They are steep, you know," Jonathan said.

"I don't think I want to come back and watch the man work," Celia said, shivering with fright.

Everyone silently moved ahead, down the steps, and toward the open outside door.

As they neared the bottom, Mandie thought she heard something outside. "I believe someone is out there," she said. "The man is probably here already to do the work." She tried to see past Joe and Senator Morton, who were ahead of her.

"Possibly," the senator agreed.

Just as she stepped outside behind Joe and the senator, she was sure she saw another flash through the woods. She set down her lantern, raised her long skirts, and hurried off into the thicket in that direction.

"Mandie, where are you going?" Joe called after her.

She didn't answer. Suddenly she met up with Polly Cornwallis, who finally stopped when she realized she had been seen.

"Polly, what are you doing down here?" Mandie asked.

Polly wouldn't look at her but kept glancing off to her left. "Looking for you," she said.

The others had followed Mandie and were now listening to the conversation.

"How did you know I was down here?" Mandie asked.

"Well, I didn't really," Polly said. "You see, a—friend—of mine wanted to see your tunnel."

"A friend of yours wanted to see our tunnel?" Mandie asked. "You know the tunnel is kept locked." She looked around and said, "And where is this friend of yours? Who is it?"

"He's from Raleigh," Polly said, quickly moving back out into the open.

"From Raleigh?" Mandie asked.

"Who is this friend from Raleigh?" Joe asked. "Do we know him?"

"He is actually my cousin and just happened to come visit us," Polly replied.

Suddenly a tall young man walked out into the open from the cluster of bushes nearby. "I'm Chester Wardell from Raleigh. Polly had offered to show me your tunnel," he said, holding his hand out to Mandie.

Mandie stepped back without shaking hands and looked at him. "I haven't heard of any cousin of Polly's from Raleigh."

The young man shuffled his feet and said, "Well, you see—"

Joe suddenly straightened up, stepped forward, and said, "Now I recognize your name. You are a reporter for the newspaper in Raleigh. Just what are you doing here? This is private property."

"I really am Polly's cousin, and I only wanted—" the young man started to say.

Mandie cut in angrily, facing him, "A newspaper reporter? I don't care if you are Polly's cousin. You get off our property this very minute, and don't you dare ever come back here, you understand? Now get going."

The young people looked at Mandie and

instantly understood why she was angry. They joined in the assault of words.

Finally Senator Morton said loudly, "I would warn you, young man, that you must leave this property immediately, or I'm sure Mr. Shaw will take legal action."

"I wasn't doing anything. I only wanted to see your tunnel," he argued.

"Yes, so you can print our personal business in your newspaper and tell the world about it," Mandie argued. Turning to Polly, she added, "And I don't think you had better show your face at our house any time soon. You know that this is private family business."

Polly turned and fled through the woods. The young man took one last look at Mandie and followed her.

Mandie just stood there, stomping her foot. "Uncle John told us to keep all this about the tunnel private. I knew Polly would get hold of it and tell everyone everything she knew," she said angrily.

"At least it's not your fault," Joe said, stepping over to her. "Come on. Let's get back to the house."

"Yes, let's get back to the house so I can tell Uncle John what's happened," Mandie said, starting up the hill.

A newspaperman from Raleigh! How did the news get that far that fast? Mandie was sure Polly had contacted him and asked him to come down. Somehow, she was going to get to the bottom of this.

Chapter 7 / Investigations

When they got back to the house, Mandie rushed into the kitchen ahead of her friends and Senator Morton. John Shaw was still sitting at the table, drinking coffee.

"Uncle John, Polly told a newspaperman from Raleigh about the tunnel, and—" she began in a loud, excited voice.

John Shaw interrupted, "What are you talking about, Amanda?" He frowned at her outburst.

"We caught Polly and this reporter—" Mandie began to explain.

Suddenly Uncle Ned, her father's old Cherokee Indian friend, who had promised to look after her when her father died, came in from outside and stepped forward to put a hand on Mandie's shoulder. "Calm down, Papoose," he told her.

Mandie pulled away from his hand and continued, "Uncle John, you told us not to talk about the tunnel, but then Polly found out about it and went and told a newspaper reporter from Raleigh, and then—"

"A newspaper reporter from Raleigh?" John Shaw quickly cut in as he stood up. "I asked,

Amanda, what are you talking about?"

"There's a reporter from the Raleigh newspaper with Polly, and she told him about the tunnel, and he tried to get us to let him in the tunnel, and we ran him off," Mandie said in one big breath.

There was complete silence in the room until John finally said, "Who is this reporter?"

"Polly said he's her cousin. Uncle John, Polly tells everything she knows and even adds to it most of the time," Mandie said.

"Where is this reporter? Where did he go?" John Shaw asked as he paced about the kitchen.

"We ran him and Polly off. They left together, so I suppose he's at Polly's house," Mandie said.

"I'm glad at least that he didn't get inside the tunnel," John Shaw said. Looking over at Uncle Ned, he said, "Uncle Ned, we need to post a guard at the door while the man is repairing the crack to be sure no one goes inside."

The old Indian nodded and said, "Two braves come with Cliff. Wait now for us to go to tunnel."

"Oh, they are already here," John Shaw said. "Then let's go get started." He walked toward the open back door.

Mandie and her friends followed the adults out into the yard. Three young Cherokee men were standing by a wagon. The eldest of the three stepped forward to shake hands with John Shaw.

"We are ready to begin work, sir," the man said.

"We'll go down with you and open up the tunnel," John Shaw told him.

Joe held up the key. "Here is the key, Mr. Shaw," he said, "and do you want to use the lanterns we have?" He looked at the young Cherokee man.

"No, we have plenty of lanterns, thank you," the young man replied.

"Then we'll just put them back where we found them," Joe said.

John Shaw took the key, and the men started down the hill for the tunnel entrance. Senator Morton and Uncle Ned went with them.

"Jonathan, I just noticed your father was with the Cherokee men," Mandie said, watching the wagon roll on in the direction of the entrance to the tunnel.

"Yes, I saw him talking to one of the Cherokee men," Jonathan said. "I wonder if he and all the other men are going to stay down there with the repair crew while they work."

"I doubt it," Mandie said. "For one thing, they haven't even had their breakfast yet, and neither have we. Let's go see if Aunt Lou is cooking it yet."

All the young people went back inside to the kitchen. Aunt Lou had just come into the room and was beginning preparations for the morning meal.

"Oh, Aunt Lou, we are all starving," Jonathan told the woman with a big grin. "One of your great big biscuits and bacon and eggs would help that situation a lot."

Aunt Lou grinned at him and said, "Oh, you quit dat now. You knows we'se gwine have all dat and more cooked in two shakes of a sheep's tail. And if y'all behave nice, I'll even allow y'all to eat it at my table over dere." She went over to the cookstove and started moving pots and pans about.

"Oh, thank you, Aunt Lou. We really appreciate your kindness," Jonathan said as he continued teasing the woman.

"Oh, Jonathan, if you don't stop that you may

cause Aunt Lou to change her mind," Mandie said, going to sit at the table.

Liza came into the kitchen to help Aunt Lou prepare the meal, and it was soon on the table.

While they ate, the young people discussed the events at the tunnel.

"Do you think that reporter may come back and try to get into the tunnel?" Jonathan asked, looking at the others around the table.

"I doubt it, because if Polly sees Uncle John down there, she won't dare come near him," Mandie said, drinking her coffee.

"Liza, go check on dat parlor. See who done got up," Aunt Lou told the girl.

Liza left the kitchen.

"I imagine everyone else is up by now," Mandie said, and looking at Aunt Lou, she asked, "Do you think we could have coffee or something in the dining room with my mother and the others?"

Aunt Lou grinned at her and said, "Sho' 'nuff, my chile. I knows you wants to hear what dey all sayin' when dey gits together. We fix it."

Liza came back into the kitchen and reported, "Everybody be in de parlor. And dey all hungry."

"We's got de food ready, Liza; just he'p me take it to de sideboard in de dinin' room. And, my chile, finish yo' food, and we take de coffee in dere."

Mandie and her friends were already finished with the food. Liza set dishes in the dining room, and when the adults were called to breakfast, Mandie and her friends went to join them.

Mandie noticed that her uncle John, Mr. Guyer, the senator, and Uncle Ned had all returned without coming through the kitchen and were in the dining room for their breakfast with Dr. and Mrs. Woodard,

Mandie's mother, Celia's mother, and Mrs. Taft. No one was talking about the tunnel. They were all discussing a dinner to which they had been invited for that night.

Jonathan said in a loud whisper to the other young people, "They are all going out tonight. What can we do that's exciting?"

"We could watch the tunnel to see if Polly and that reporter come back," Mandie said.

"Couldn't we think up something else to do?" Celia asked. "I don't think I want to go down there in the dark tonight."

"I don't suppose it would be a good idea to go down there at night," Mandie replied.

"We could play checkers," Joe suggested.

"But this is just breakfast time. We have all day to do something before tonight when they all go out," Celia reminded them.

"You're right," Jonathan agreed.

"So while it's still daytime we could always check on Polly and that reporter," Mandie told them.

"And how do you plan to do that?" Jonathan asked.

"We could just walk around all over our property and go over to the line where our land joins the Cornwallises' and watch for them. They are bound to be moving around somewhere or other. That man won't just sit still now that he has come all the way from Raleigh," Mandie explained.

"But he might have gone on back to Raleigh when he couldn't get in the tunnel," Joe said.

"Maybe your uncle would let us go look when the men finish repairing the crack in the tunnel," Jonathan suggested.

The adults were finishing their meal and were

getting up to leave the room. Mandie looked at them and told her friends, "Let's go out in the yard."

The young people left the table quickly as everyone got up, and Mandie led the way out into the backyard. They sat down on a bench under a huge chestnut tree.

"From here we can see everyone going and coming from the house," Mandie explained. "I'd like to know when the men have finished repairing the tunnel wall. Somehow we might get a chance to look at it."

As she was talking, one of the young Cherokee workmen came hurrying up the hill toward the house. She watched to see where he was going and was surprised when he came toward them and spoke to her.

"We need to speak with Mr. Shaw," he said. "We have some unexpected problems in the tunnel. Do you know where he is?"

Mandie quickly stood up and said, "Yes, he's in the house. Come on. I'll get him." She hurried toward the back door.

John Shaw, Lindall Guyer, Uncle Ned, Senator Morton, and Dr. Woodard all came out onto the back porch as they approached.

"Uncle John, this man wants to speak to you," she called to her uncle.

The men stopped and waited until Mandie and the Cherokee workman got to the porch.

"Sir, Cliff has sent me to tell you we have a problem with the crack in the tunnel and need for you to come look," the young fellow said.

John Shaw looked alarmed and said quickly, "Of course. I'll be right there."

The young fellow hurried back down the hill and

disappeared in the trees toward the entrance to the tunnel.

"Let me get an extra lantern in case we need one," John Shaw told the other men and went back inside the house.

Mandie watched while the other men waited on the porch, and John Shaw quickly rejoined them with a lantern in his hand. The group hurriedly walked down the hill toward the tunnel.

Mandie quickly motioned to her friends in the yard to follow. They stayed far enough behind that the men wouldn't notice them.

"What is wrong?" Joe asked.

"I don't know. Let's go find out," Mandie told him.

"I'll go with y'all to the entrance, but I don't want to go back inside that tunnel," Celia said.

"Oh, Celia, something exciting is happening. Don't you want to go see for yourself what it is?" Jonathan teased her as he walked by her side.

Mandie slowed down to give the men time to enter the tunnel; then she hurried forward and stopped at the entrance.

"Are we going inside?" Jonathan asked.

"Maybe, maybe not," Mandie replied, trying to see inside the dark tunnel from the doorway. She could hear voices in there but could not understand what they were saying.

The young people stayed there, listening for a long time and waiting for someone to come out. Finally the same young man who had come for John Shaw came outside to get something out of their wagon, which was parked near the entrance. He started back for the tunnel.

"Could you tell us what has happened?" Mandie

quickly asked him as he walked by her.

He stopped, frowned, and looked at her. "The crack got much larger when we tried to clean it for the mortar," he said. "I am sorry, but we are in a hurry."

As the young fellow quickly reentered the tunnel, Mandie turned to her friends and asked, "Did y'all hear that? That crack got bigger."

"Let's sit down over there," Joe suggested, pointing to a log bench under a tree at the edge of the woods. He led the way to it.

As they sat down, Jonathan said, "If that crack is opening up, it could be dangerous."

"But it could have been just mortar that was already loose," Mandie said. "Remember, Senator Morton said the loose mortar around it would have to be cleared away."

"But that fellow seemed excited, as though something was definitely wrong," Celia said.

"Maybe if we just sit and wait and listen we can find out exactly what is going on in there," Joe told them.

They waited and waited, and it seemed as though no one was ever going to come out of the tunnel. Finally Dr. Woodard came out alone.

Joe jumped up and hurried over to his father and asked, "What is wrong inside? Is the tunnel cracking open more than it was?"

"Yes, I suppose you'd say that's what it's doing," Dr. Woodard replied as the others gathered around him to listen. "I have to go make a round of calls and can't stay to see what happens. However, it seems the crack is widening, and from what we could see, there must be some kind of door or wall behind the tunnel wall."

"A door? Or wall?" Mandie repeated in excitement.

"Now, you young people stay out here. I don't think Mr. Shaw would want you in the way in there," Dr. Woodard said, turning to walk on. "I'll be back later this afternoon. I have to go up the mountain to see old Mrs. Fortner. And while I'm up there, I'll check on another two or three older folk." He continued up the hill toward the house.

The young people looked at each other and excitedly discussed the new situation in the tunnel.

"I hope Uncle John investigates whatever is behind the crack and doesn't just fill up the crack and close it," Mandie said.

"But what if it's too dangerous to open it up enough to look inside?" Celia asked.

"They must not think it's dangerous to the house foundation, or they would be having everyone leave the house," Jonathan said.

"I wish I could see it," Joe said.

"Yes, I'd like to see it, too," Mandie said. "Whenever Uncle John does come back out, I'm going to ask him all about it."

"And he's going to tell us we can't go inside the tunnel," Celia reminded her.

"At least he could explain what's going on," Mandie replied.

There was a sudden sound of something going through the brush behind them. The four quickly turned to stare at the woods.

"I believe there's someone in there," Mandie said under her breath.

"Yes, it sounded like someone running through there," Joe agreed.

"Come on, Joe, let's go look," Jonathan told

him and then added, "You girls stay here and watch the door of the tunnel and see that no one goes inside." He hurried off through the woods.

"Be sure you stay alert," Joe told the girls as he rushed off after Jonathan.

Mandie and Celia looked at each other.

As soon as the boys were out of sight, Mandie heard something in the bushes again. She became very still and waited and watched. The noise moved on and grew dimmer and disappeared altogether.

"Do you think that was someone then?" Celia asked.

"Yes, it didn't sound like an animal," Mandie decided, "but I was afraid to go investigate because Uncle John and the others might come out of the tunnel and I'd miss them."

"Maybe Joe and Jonathan will find whoever it was," Celia said, shivering slightly. "I don't like scary things like that."

It seemed to Mandie that everything was moving awfully slowly. The boys should have returned by now. She got up and walked around. And someone inside the tunnel should have come out for some reason by now. Everything was at a standstill, and there was really nothing she could do about it.

"Do you think Joe and Jonathan got lost?" Celia finally asked.

Mandie stopped walking to look at her. "I don't think so," she said. "They are probably chasing someone around and around in the woods and haven't been able to catch up with them."

Then the girls finally saw some of the men coming out of the tunnel. John Shaw was walking along with the senator, Mr. Guyer, and Uncle Ned as they talked.

"I'll go on with Cliff to get the supplies and will see y'all later at the house," John Shaw said as Cliff came out and got in his wagon. John Shaw got in with him.

The other men walked on up the hill toward the house.

"All those men came out and didn't even see us," Mandie said, blowing out her breath. She stopped and looked at Celia and asked, "Want to go inside the tunnel while they're gone?"

"There are two more Cherokee men who didn't come out, Mandie," Celia reminded her.

"I know," she replied. "That's why I am not afraid to go inside. They are there. Are you coming?"

"No, I believe I'll just stay here and watch for Joe and Jonathan," Celia said. "They won't know where you are."

"All right. I won't be but a few minutes," Mandie promised as she hurried toward the entrance of the tunnel.

Someone had left a lighted lantern inside not very far from the door. Mandie hurriedly picked it up and continued up the passageway in the tunnel. She couldn't hear a sound, but she knew the two workmen had not come out. Therefore, they must still be inside somewhere.

She finally heard a slight metallic noise, like tools being moved around, and as she got farther inside she saw lighted lanterns ahead, revealing the two workmen mixing something in buckets. Not wanting to startle them, she called ahead. "I came to see the crack," she said. "I won't disturb your work. It'll only take a few minutes to look."

She hurried on forward and came up to the two

men. They looked at her in surprise and didn't say anything.

"Is there some new problem with the crack?" she asked them.

One of the men was the one she had spoken to before. He shrugged his shoulders and replied, "It may not be a problem. We maybe can fix it."

"Would you please show me what you are talking about?" Mandie asked as she slowly continued toward them.

"Yes, here, look," the man said. "The crack gets wider and wider." The man walked over to the wall and flashed his lantern on it.

Mandie gasped in surprise. The crack was indeed much wider than it had been when she saw it before. She leaned to look closely. And there did seem to be something behind it. She reached her hand out to stick her finger in the crack and then remembered that she had almost got it stuck before. So she leaned closer and held the lantern up where it would shine into the crack.

"What do you think it is in there?" she turned to ask the man.

"Perhaps a door, or another wall," the man said. "Mr. Shaw must decide whether to open it and investigate or close it up for good."

"Oh, I hope he opens it to see what's back there," Mandie told the man.

"Mr. Shaw also said we were not to let anyone come in here, so we must ask you to go back outside," the man said.

"All right. I just wanted to see what things looked like now that you had begun work on it," Mandie replied. "Thank you." She turned and started back out of the tunnel.

She would love to talk to Uncle John about the crack and tell him that he must open it up to see what was behind it or whatever it was would be lost forever. However, she knew she was not supposed to go inside the tunnel. So what could she do about it? She would discuss it with her friends and see what they thought about the situation. She rushed back outside to find them.

Chapter 8 / Delays

When Mandie came out of the tunnel, she saw that Joe and Jonathan had returned and were talking to Celia. She hurried to join them and sat down.

"You went in the tunnel?" Joe asked in surprise.

"There are two of the workmen in there, and all I did was look," Mandie replied. Then she excitedly added, "The crack is getting bigger. I could probably have stuck my finger through it, but I was afraid it would get stuck—"

"You didn't, I hope," Celia interrupted.

"Could you see through the crack?" Jonathan asked.

"Yes, a little, enough to tell there is something behind it, either another wall or a door, or something, anyhow," Mandie told her friends. "And Uncle John has just got to open the crack up and see what it is behind it. If he seals over it, we will never know what it is on the other side."

"What is he planning on doing?" Joe asked.

"I don't know," Mandie said. "The man inside told me Uncle John had to let them know what to do further on the crack, open it up and see what's behind it or go ahead and seal it up."

"Did the man say when your uncle would let them know?" Jonathan asked.

"Celia told us your uncle went off with Cliff to get some supplies. Do you know when he will return?" Joe asked.

"No, I didn't ask the man inside," Mandie said. "But they are stopping work until he does return, so I imagine he won't be gone long." Then she remembered that the boys had gone investigating a noise they had heard in the woods. "Did y'all find anyone in the woods?"

"No, not even an animal," Joe replied. "And we didn't hear a sound, either."

"I wonder where that reporter went," Mandie said. "Did y'all see Polly anywhere while y'all were searching the woods? Did you go near her house?"

"We went across the back line of their property, but we didn't see anyone there," Joe said.

Cliff returned in his wagon with John Shaw. The young people watched as they unloaded two large croker sacks full of something and carried them into the tunnel. Mandie and her friends were far enough away in the trees that the men did not see them.

"I wonder what they had in those sacks," Mandie said.

"Whatever it was, it was heavy," Celia added.

In a few minutes John Shaw and Cliff came back out of the tunnel and stood at the entrance talking until the other workmen came outside. Then John locked the door and started up the hill as the others went to the wagon.

"I'll see you bright and early tomorrow morning," John Shaw said, waving to Cliff as the man drove up the hill to the road.

As soon as everyone was out of sight, Mandie

said, "Well, we might as well leave, too,"

"It's probably time to eat," Jonathan said, grinning at her.

"Probably," Mandie agreed as they all started up the hill toward the house.

"I wonder why they quit work," Joe remarked as they walked along.

Mandie stopped and looked at him, "Maybe Uncle John is going to open the crack and they wouldn't have had time to do it today and close it back up because the workmen were only supposed to seal up the crack when they came."

"You are probably right," Joe agreed.

"But how are we going to find out what they are planning to do?" Mandie asked.

"Just ask," Jonathan told her.

"No, we can't do that because then Uncle John would know that we have been talking to the workmen," Mandie replied.

"I suppose we'll just have to listen to their conversations, then," Jonathan said.

When they got to the back of the house, Liza was coming out the back door. She was carrying a bucket of water, which she poured on plants growing nearby.

"Liza, is everybody ready to eat?" Mandie asked.

"Lawsy mercy, no, Missy Amanda," Liza replied. "Ain't got it all cooked yet. Lots of people to feed." She turned to go back in the door.

Mandie turned to her friends and said, "Let's go sit in the arbor."

"That would be a nice restful place after all those weeds and bushes we've been in this morning," Celia said.

The four young people sat down under the arbor and were silent for a while. Then suddenly Celia whispered, "Look, there's your grandmother, Mandie, with Jonathan's father." She motioned down the pathway.

Mandie straightened up and looked. Her grandmother and Mr. Guyer were walking slowly up the path, pausing now and then to talk. When they came to a bench on the other side of the walkway, they sat down.

Mandie held her breath, hoping the two didn't see her and her friends. She couldn't hear everything they were saying, and she didn't want to eavesdrop, but it was too late to make her presence known.

Mrs. Taft was saying, "No, Lin, it's too late to pick up where we left off years and years ago."

"I disagree. It's never too late if you love someone," Lindall Guyer replied.

The young people couldn't see them because of shrubbery down the pathway, but they could hear most of what was said.

"Would you please tell me one thing?" Lindall Guyer said. "Do you plan on marrying the senator?"

Mandie caught her breath and strained to listen.

"To be rude to a rude question, Lindall, that is none of your business," Mrs. Taft replied.

Mandie saw Jonathan grinning at her.

"But I don't consider that a rude question," Mr. Guyer replied. "The answer is very important to me because if you don't have serious plans with Senator Morton, then I can keep trying," Lindall Guyer said with a little laugh.

"But you won't have much chance to do that," Mrs. Taft said. "Because I doubt if I'll ever go to your house again. I only went this time to get things settled in my mind once and for all."

"But we're still friends; therefore I can come visit at your house," Mr. Guyer told her.

"It wouldn't do you any good, Lin," Mrs. Taft said. "You should find some nice young woman and get married again yourself."

"I don't want a nice young woman," he said. "I'm not young myself, and I certainly don't want to get involved with a young woman." He cleared his throat loudly. "We used to have a lot in common, and I believe we still do. Maybe you are thinking about my work. I am gone for long periods of time, and I am sometimes involved in danger for the government. However, I am planning to retire soon. And if you would marry me, I would retire immediately."

"Maybe I've become so used to my freedom without a husband that I don't want to get tied down again," Mrs. Taft said.

"Oh, so then you are not planning on marrying the senator," Mr. Guyer quickly said with a loud chuckle. "Maybe I have a chance."

"Oh, let's discontinue this silly conversation. I need to get back to the house and freshen up before the meal is served," Mrs. Taft said.

The young people quickly and silently darted behind the rosebushes as Mrs. Taft and Mr. Guyer came within sight on their way up the pathway.

As soon as they were gone, Mandie told her friends, "Oh, I feel absolutely, positively terrible, listening to all that private conversation."

The four came back out of the bushes and sat down.

"I thought that was an exciting conversation," Jonathan said with a big grin. "Now we know my father is still in love with your grandmother, Mandie."

"Maybe he just thinks he is. It has been a long time since they were young," Mandie reminded him.

"Ah, but true love never dies," Jonathan said, dramatically placing his hand over his heart.

Mandie laughed and looked at her friends when they didn't.

"I believe that," Joe said seriously. "True love never dies."

"I do, too," Celia quickly added.

"You see," Jonathan said, "I must be right about that."

"Anyhow, if my grandmother is going to get married again, I would prefer she marry the senator," Mandie said with a smirk.

Jonathan looked at her with his mouth open. "You don't like my father? And here I thought we might get to be kinpeople one day," he said.

"I didn't say I don't like your father, Jonathan," Mandie replied. "It's just that my grandmother always has to be the boss, and Senator Morton lets her do that. So if she married him she would have someone to boss around, and maybe she would stop trying to plan everything in my life."

"But, Mandie," Celia said, "I'd think she would be able to boss Jonathan's father around, because he is the one begging right now."

"Maybe, but I've never known anyone who could just take over with my father," Jonathan said.

Joe cleared his throat and said, "You are all forgetting. A real marriage should be a two-sided affair, not one a boss and the other a follower."

Mandie looked at him thoughtfully and said, "I never had thought about marriage that way. I always thought one or the other was the boss."

"My mother and father get along just fine.

Neither one bosses the other," Joe explained.

"Jonathan, your father married your mother, and he must have loved her. He didn't pursue my grandmother then," Mandie said.

"I suppose so, but you know I can't remember her, and their love, or whatever it was, didn't last long because she died," Jonathan said.

"Anyhow, I don't think my grandmother will marry your father, Jonathan," Mandie decided as she stood up. "Let's go back to the house now."

"You may be wrong," Jonathan told her as the four started uphill toward the house.

When the four young people went inside the house, there was no one in sight. They looked in the parlor and found it empty.

Then they went to their rooms to freshen up, with agreement among them to meet back at the top of the main staircase in fifteen minutes.

"I suppose everyone else has gone to their rooms, too," Celia remarked as she brushed her long auburn hair and tied it back with a ribbon.

"I reckon," Mandie absentmindedly replied. She quickly brushed her blond hair. "You know, I've always wondered what my grandfather Taft was like, whether Grandmother was able to boss him around."

"I wouldn't think so, Mandie. After all, he was a United States senator," Celia reminded her. "I imagine he exuded a lot of bossy power himself. She did say down there by the arbor that she enjoyed being free without a husband."

"I suppose I'm a lot like my grandmother. I don't want someone bossing me around," Mandie replied, stepping over to the floor-length mirror in the corner to look at herself. Shaking out the folds in her long skirt, she flipped around to look at Celia and added, "Therefore, I don't think I ever want to get married."

Celia turned to look at her and said with a grin, "But Joe said neither one should be the boss, which means that he wouldn't try to boss you around if you married him."

Mandie stomped her foot and said, "Celia, stop that. We are too young to be talking about getting married. We'd better be talking about what college we are going to next year." She gave her long skirt a swish and started toward the door. "Come on, let's go."

Joe and Jonathan were sitting on the bench at the top of the staircase.

The boys stood up as the girls approached.

"My, my," Jonathan said with a grin. "What took you girls so long? I can't see a thing different about you."

Snowball came running down the hallway and jumped upon the top of the banister along the steps.

"Snowball, get down from there before you fall and break your neck," Mandie yelled at the white cat.

Snowball stopped and looked at his mistress. Mandie stepped over and quickly picked him up. Turning to her friends, she said, "Come on, I'm going to take him to the kitchen, which will give us an excuse to see if Aunt Lou knows anything about what Uncle John is planning to do with that crack in the wall." She started down the steps. The others followed.

"Do you have to have an excuse to go to the kitchen?" Jonathan asked.

Mandie looked back at him and replied, "Yes, right now I do because Aunt Lou is busy getting the food ready for all our company, and that's about a dozen people, which is a big job." She went on down the staircase and waited for her friends to catch up with her.

"Mandie, I haven't seen Jenny, your cook, today," Celia remarked.

"She has gone to visit her sister down in Georgia, who is recovering from a bad fall, but she'll be back soon," Mandie told her.

"Isn't she Abraham's wife?" Jonathan asked.

"Yes, and they have their own house on the property behind here," Mandie replied.

"With Aunt Lou short of help and all these people here, maybe we shouldn't bother her right now," Celia suggested.

"We won't bother her. I'll just leave Snowball in the kitchen and ask a question while I'm doing it," Mandie said.

"Maybe we could help with something or other," Joe suggested.

"That's a good idea," Jonathan said with a big grin. "But what can we do? I don't know how to cook."

Celia quickly looked at the others and said, "We could set the table. We know how to do that."

"I don't think Aunt Lou would allow it," Mandie said. "She's real bossy about her work."

Celia smiled and said, "We don't have to tell her. I know y'all keep the dishes in the china closet in the dining room, and we could slip in there and get them down and set the table. Surprise."

Mandie looked at her and then at the boys and said, "Yes, let's do that. But let me put Snowball in the kitchen first." She started on down the hallway toward the kitchen.

As soon as she pushed the door open, she set Snowball down, and he ran for his plate, which was kept near the woodbox by the big iron cookstove. Aunt Lou was putting something in the oven, and she glanced back at Mandie and her friends, who had stopped at the door. As she straightened up she said, "Now, my chile, de food not ready yet, and we busy right now."

Liza was chopping something on the cook table. "And we ain't got no time fo' y'all," she said.

"I just wanted to bring Snowball to eat. I didn't know whether he had even had his breakfast or not," Mandie said, smiling. "Did you see the men who were working in the tunnel when they left, Aunt Lou?"

"No, I ain't had time to see nobody," Aunt Lou replied. "And I ain't got time to see y'all, either, right now, so git. We'se busy." She fanned her big white apron in their direction.

Mandie's friends quickly backed out into the hall-way. Mandie followed them as she said, "Yes, ma'am, we're going."

Outside in the hallway, and with the kitchen door closed, Mandie turned to her friends and said, "All right, we'll have to be quiet so Aunt Lou won't hear us." She pushed open the door to the dining room down the hall.

With all four of the young people helping, it didn't take long to get dishes down and set on the long table, and then the silverware and napkins. Mandie carefully straightened everything and stood back to look over their work.

"Aunt Lou is going to be surprised," Celia said.

"Yes, and we'd better make ourselves scarce, as she says, when she finds out what we've done. Let's go see if anyone is in the parlor," Mandie said, opening the door to the hall.

The parlor was empty, but by the time they had all sat down, the adults began coming in. Mandie tried to listen to the conversation around the room, hoping the adults would discuss the crack in the tunnel, but there seemed to be several different subjects being discussed, and it was hard to hear most of it.

"Your grandmother is not having much to say," Jonathan whispered to Mandie.

Mandie smiled as she looked at Mrs. Taft, who was seated across the room on a settee between Senator Morton and Mr. Guyer. The two men seemed to be talking to each other without any input from her.

Glancing at her mother, Elizabeth Shaw, who was talking with Mrs. Woodard and Jane Hamilton, Mandie distinctly heard her say, "Yes, I'm going to have to insist that Amanda make a decision about college soon."

"It would be nice if the girls would go to Joe's school. We could all visit there together," Mrs. Woodard said.

"I think Celia is going to decide on the one near us," Jane Hamilton told them.

Mandie quickly looked at Celia, who had also been listening to the conversation.

Celia said, "Now, Mandie, I have not made any decision. Mother would like for me to go to school near home."

"Celia Hamilton, you can't desert me where I have to go to a strange school all by myself," Mandie told her.

"The very solution would be to go to my school," Joe reminded the girls.

"Now, we could settle the whole dispute without any hard feelings if you girls would just come up to New York to school," Jonathan said with a big grin.

At that moment Liza appeared in the doorway and said loudly, "Miz Lizbeth, de food on de table." Then, stepping inside to look at Mandie and her friends, she added with a big grin, "And de dishes done been put on de table, too."

Mandie tried to keep a sober face as she replied, "Really? How did they get there?"

"One of dem li'l fairies musta done it," Liza replied and danced on out of the room.

Elizabeth rose and led the way to the dining room. The young people followed.

Aunt Lou was in the dining room, placing food on the sideboard. She turned to whisper to Mandie as she passed by her, "I'se gwine to spank you where you sits down if you don't stay outta my business, my chile."

Mandie grinned at her and said, "Then you will have to spank all four of us, and I don't think you would be able to manage that."

"You'd be surprised whut I kin do; you'd be surprised," the old woman replied as she left the room, shaking her head.

Everyone seemed to be hungry, and they were all eating instead of talking. The only conversation Mandie could overhear was about the adults' dinner that night with the Campbells, friends of the Shaws.

Mandie whispered to her friends, "I wish Uncle John would discuss the crack in the tunnel."

Joe whispered back, "He's not doing that because he knows you are listening." He grinned at her.

Mandie smiled at him and said, as she blew out

her breath, "Oh well, I'll find out what's going on sooner or later."

And she meant it. She just had to know what was behind that crack in the tunnel.

Chapter 9 / Undecided

The afternoon dragged for Mandie and her friends. The women stayed in their rooms most of the afternoon, getting ready for the night's visit out to supper. The men sat around in the backyard, talking about everything but the tunnel, from what Mandie and her friends could overhear as they constantly walked in and out of the house in an effort to eavesdrop.

Then Dr. Woodard returned from visiting his patients. Mandie and Celia were sitting on the back porch steps. Joe and Jonathan were leaning against the posts.

"I'm glad to find you all here together," Dr. Woodard said as he stopped his buggy in the driveway near the men. He stepped down and went over to join the men.

"I'm glad you have returned, Dr. Woodard," John Shaw told him. "Sit down." He indicated a bench nearby.

Dr. Woodard sat down and continued, "I've been over to see old Mrs. Fortner, and I think she's going to be all right, just the sniffles, really. But she has a problem. The fence around her chicken yard is down. Some of the posts look like they've rotted. And she lives alone, a long way from any neighbors, and her chickens have all got out and scattered through the woods."

John Shaw quickly said, "Do you think we might be able to redo her fence?"

"Yes, that's exactly what I was going to suggest," Dr. Woodard replied. He looked around at the other men, Senator Morton, Lindall Guyer, and Uncle Ned. "Would any of you like to run back over there with me and see what we can do about that fence?"

"Of course," Senator Morton replied.

"Yes," Uncle Ned said, nodding.

"I'm ready right now," Mr. Guyer told him.

They all stood up as John Shaw said, "Let's get some tools out of the barn." Then, turning back to Dr. Woodard, he asked, "Is the fence wire useable?"

"Oh, yes, it's fine for a while at least," Dr. Woodard said. "It's the posts that have rotted down and fallen."

"Then we'll load up some wood and take it with us," John Shaw said, walking on back toward the barn.

The other men followed.

Mandie and her friends had overheard the conversation.

Joe looked at the others and said, "I think perhaps I ought to volunteer to help."

"I will, too," Jonathan added.

"I can do something," Mandie said, standing up.

"I'll go, too, then, if you are all going," Celia said as she rose from the steps.

Mandie frowned at her friends and said, "We will have to get Uncle John's permission to go, you know."

"Yes," Celia said.

The boys nodded in agreement.

The four walked over to the door of the barn, where the men were getting supplies ready.

"Uncle John," Mandie began, "do you think we could go, too? Maybe there is something we can do."

John Shaw looked up from the boards he was stacking and shook his head as he replied, "No, Amanda, thank you, but we men can take care of this. Just remember to tell your mother where we have gone if she comes downstairs before we return."

"Yes, we shouldn't be gone long," Dr. Woodard added, picking up a bag of nails from a shelf.

Joe looked at his father and said, "Dad, I would be glad to help."

"I know, son, but we have plenty of help here," Dr. Woodard told him. "And I'll depend on you to explain to your mother where we've gone."

"Yes, sir," Joe replied. He looked at the other three young people and said, "I don't think we are needed. Let's find something else to do." He left the barn, and the others followed.

The four stood around on the back porch until the men loaded their supplies into John Shaw's wagon and drove off.

"Let's go sit in the parlor," Mandie suggested.

"That's a good idea," Jonathan said with a big grin. "Because when the ladies come down, Aunt Lou will probably serve coffee, won't she?"

Mandie nodded in the affirmative and added, "And something sweet, perhaps chocolate cake."

"Then, let's hurry in there. I wouldn't want to miss that chocolate cake," Joe said.

There was no one in the parlor. Snowball was curled up on a footstool.

As they all sat down, Jonathan said, "Perhaps we should let Aunt Lou know that we are in here so she could get that coffee started."

Mandie smiled at him and said, "That coffee pot stays full at all times on Aunt Lou's stove."

"And does she keep chocolate cake made all the time?" Joe asked with a grin.

"Just about all the time, especially when she knows you are here," Mandie replied.

Liza appeared in the doorway. "Jis' checkin' to see who all's in heah," she said as she glanced around the room.

"Are you going to bring coffee, Liza?" Mandie asked.

"And chocolate cake," Jonathan added.

Liza grinned at them and said, "I has to go ask Aunt Lou." She turned to leave.

"Just tell her everyone is here who would like chocolate cake," Jonathan told her.

"All the men went off to Mrs. Fortner's, Liza, and won't be back for a while," Mandie explained.

"And where de ladies at?" Liza asked.

"As far as we know, they are all in their rooms," Mandie replied.

"Gittin' dolled up to go out tonight," Liza added with a grin and turned to go back down the hallway.

"Do you think she'll bring it?" Jonathan asked.

"Yes, Aunt Lou will send us chocolate cake and coffee," Mandie replied. "And I'm sure she knows we will be the only ones home for supper tonight."

"Since there are only four of us, do you think Aunt Lou would allow us to eat at her table in the kitchen?" Jonathan asked.

"Oh, Jonathan, that's the table she uses for her meals with Liza and the other servants," Mandie said.

"Couldn't we just eat with them, then?" Jonathan asked.

Mandie laughed and said, "No, Aunt Lou wouldn't allow it. She likes to keep everything separate between us and the servants. Besides, there wouldn't be enough room for the four of us, since there are four of them when Jenny is home."

"Where is Mr. Bond? Where does he eat when everyone goes out?" Jonathan asked. "Since he's not a servant, not a relative, but the caretaker."

"He's not here right now," Mandie said. "Uncle John sent him over to Asheville for something, and I doubt he will get back before tomorrow. I heard them talking in the hallway this morning."

In a few minutes Liza came back with the tea cart, loaded with coffee and chocolate cake. "Aunt Lou, she done tole me to bring dis heah choc'late cake, but she say fo' y'all to be in de dinin' room at six fo' suppuh, and she say don't be late," Liza explained as she poured cups of coffee and distributed them.

"Thank you, Liza," Mandie said. "Tell Aunt Lou we'll be there."

Liza finished serving the cake and coffee and left the room.

"If we eat supper at six o'clock, it will still be daylight," Jonathan said. "We could go out for a walk or something." He sipped his coffee.

"Yes, that's a good idea," Joe agreed. "I need some exercise." He took a bite of his cake.

"Is there any special place y'all want to walk to?" Celia asked.

"Just walk, I suppose," Jonathan said.

"No place in particular," Joe added.

"We could go down and check the outside entrance to the tunnel," Mandie suggested.

"Now, Mandie, you know your uncle keeps that door locked," Joe reminded her.

"There's always a possibility that he might forget to sometime," Mandie said. "And we still don't know what Uncle John is going to do about that crack. I haven't heard a single word about it."

"Why don't you just ask him, in a nice way, of course?" Jonathan suggested.

Mandie quickly looked at him and said, "I don't want to irritate him. And then, too, he may not ever let us look at the crack, especially now that it is opening up and could be dangerous."

The men weren't gone long. When they returned they went to their rooms, changed clothes, and returned to the parlor, where Liza was again serving coffee.

"Did y'all get the fence back up?" Joe asked his father.

"Yes, it didn't take long with all of us working on it, and I believe it will stay awhile now," Dr. Woodard told him. "We weren't able to find all the chickens, though. We rounded up twenty-three, and Mrs. Fortner said there should have been about fifty."

"Yes, it's too bad that many got away, but like I told her, I'll take more to her as soon as I find someone who has some for sale," John Shaw added.

"What plans do you young people have for tonight while we older ones are out?" Lindall Guyer asked Jonathan.

Jonathan shrugged his shoulders and replied, "Nothing in particular. We are going for a walk."

Glancing at John Shaw, he added, "We would like to see the crack in the tunnel if Mr. Shaw would allow it."

Mandie quickly held her breath as she watched her uncle.

John Shaw quickly spoke up. "No, not unless I'm with y'all. It could be dangerous because it is getting wider."

Jonathan cleared his throat and said, "Well, then, Mr. Shaw, do you think we might be able to see it tomorrow when you have time?"

"We'll see," John Shaw said, and turning to Dr. Woodard, he said, "Cliff will be back early tomorrow morning, and I'll have to decide by then whether to seal it up or open the crack and see what's behind it."

"Any idea as to what you might decide?" Dr. Woodard asked.

"Well, it would be much easier to just seal it up, which wouldn't take long," John Shaw said. "However, not knowing what's behind it, I'm not sure it would be a good idea to do that. We probably need to see what's back there. And, of course, that would take a lot more time and a lot more work, depending on what we would find."

Dr. Woodard cleared his throat and said, "If it were my house, I wouldn't be satisfied until I found out what is behind it. There could be some faulty foundation work in there that needs repairing. We just don't know what that tornado did when it went through here."

"Yes, I suppose I'd always worry about it if I don't find out what's back there," John Shaw said thoughtfully.

Mandie waited to hear more, but John Shaw

changed the topic of the conversation. She looked at Jonathan and grinned. He had some nerve, asking her uncle about seeing the crack.

The men's conversation had come back around to the chickens for Mrs. Fortner.

"I know where chickens can be bought," Uncle Ned spoke up.

"You do, Uncle Ned?" John Shaw replied.

"Yes, Cherokee man over mountain sell chickens," the old man said.

"I can't go over there tomorrow because the workmen are coming back and I need to be here whenever they continue work on the crack," John Shaw said. "But when they finish, and it may take them several days, then I can go with you to see about the chickens."

Dr. Woodard looked at the young people and then back at John Shaw as he said, "I will be busy making more calls tomorrow, but perhaps Joe could go with Uncle Ned to get the chickens."

"I'd be glad to go," Joe spoke up.

"But then we will have to take them up to Mrs. Fortner, and that will take time," John Shaw said.

"If Uncle Ned wants to deliver them to the lady, I'll go with him up there," Joe said.

John Shaw turned to Uncle Ned and asked, "Where is this place located? Is it anywhere near Mrs. Fortner?"

"No, other side of mountain," the old man replied. "Make two trips, one to get chickens and one to take to Mrs. Fortner."

"Unless we are going home tomorrow, I have plenty of time to do that," Joe told his father.

"I thought we'd stay until that crack is safely taken care of just in case I'm needed here," Dr.

Woodard said. "Go ahead and plan this with Uncle Ned if you want to."

Mandie listened as Uncle Ned and Joe made plans to leave early the next morning, get the chickens, and go on over to the other side of the mountain to deliver them to Mrs. Fortner. It would probably take all day since Uncle Ned said it was a long ways to get them.

The ladies finally came down to the parlor, and by then John Shaw said it was time for them to all leave for the Campbells'.

"I don't know how late we will be, Amanda, but don't stay up too late," Elizabeth Shaw told her.

"Yes, ma'am," Mandie replied. "We aren't doing anything in particular, anyhow."

Jane Hamilton also cautioned Celia not to sit up waiting for them to return. They would not be in a hurry to get back.

As soon as all the adults had left, the young people discussed the crack in the tunnel.

"Uncle John must think it is dangerous," Mandie decided. "I could tell he was worried about closing it up without investigating behind it, and, Joe, your father seemed to think it should be opened up."

"Yes, I listened to what they were saying," Joe agreed.

"I would say your uncle is going to look into it and not just seal it up," Jonathan said.

"I don't think I want to be in this house if they open that crack up," Celia said. "It could damage the foundation, and the house could sink or something."

"Yes, it could," Joe agreed. "However, I don't believe it would damage the whole house. This is a well-built house, even though it's old, and I don't believe that tornado did much, if any, damage to the foundation or the house would have shown signs of it somewhere before now. Also, the tunnel only runs under part of the house. The rest of the house is sitting on firm ground."

"I suppose if we just go and sit where we were today, we could watch and see them coming in and out tomorrow and maybe overhear something about the crack," Mandie told her friends.

"As long as they don't see us," Celia said. "Otherwise Mr. Shaw might ask us to leave or stop hanging around the tunnel."

Liza came to the door of the parlor and announced, "Y'all's supper be on de table. Aunt Lou say git a move on now."

"We're coming right now, Liza, thank you," Mandie said as she quickly rose from her chair.

Her friends joined her, and they all went into the dining room, where the meal was set out.

"If we don't waste too much time eating, we'll have more time before dark to go for a walk," Celia told the others as they all sat down together at the end of the table.

"Right," Jonathan agreed. "I can always eat in a hurry."

Mandie asked Joe, "Will you and Uncle Ned be gone all day tomorrow?"

Joe replied, "I'm not sure. I have no idea how long it will take us to get the chickens and deliver them to Mrs. Fortner."

"Just how are you going to pick up all those chickens and deliver them to that woman? What do you put them in or whatever? I've never hauled chickens before," Jonathan said with a grin.

"Oh, that will be easy," Joe said. "We'll just take

some cages with us if Mr. Shaw has any, and if he doesn't we'll get them from the people we are getting the chickens from. Uncle Ned's wagon will hold enough.''

"No such problems in the city of New York, where I live," Jonathan said, grinning, as he shook his head.

"You get an education every time you leave that great big city, don't you?" Joe asked him.

"Sometimes," Jonathan agreed. "Life down here is so different from ours in New York. And I've never lived in a small place like this. All the boarding schools I've been to were in large cities.''

Mandie quickly sipped her coffee and said, "I just can't imagine my grandmother ever living in New York, but evidently she did when she was young, because that was where she knew your father, Jonathan."

Jonathan grinned at her and said, "I still think they should get back together, your grandmother and my father. I wouldn't mind having your grandmother for a stepmother."

"You wouldn't?" Mandie asked in surprise. "You just don't know my grandmother, then. She can really take over everybody and everything when she wants to."

"You know that she even bought the school Mandie and I go to in Asheville, don't you?" Celia asked.

"I remember hearing something mentioned about that. But wasn't it because the old lady sisters who own it, the Misses Heathwood, were in money trouble and about to close it up?" Jonathan asked.

"Well, that was one reason, wasn't it, Mandie?" Celia replied and looked to Mandie to explain.

"It was a good excuse for her to buy it and

become the boss as the new owner," Mandie explained. "She hasn't made a whole lot of changes. Miss Hope and Miss Prudence still run it, but I'm sure they consult my grandmother on every move they make."

"After this next year, you girls will be finished with that school, and then where will you all be going to college? You have to make up your minds in time to get enrolled somewhere, you know," Joe said. "And I would highly recommend my college, where I go in New Orleans."

"Before we get into all that, let's hurry and finish our food and get outside before it gets dark," Mandie suggested, hastily eating the potatoes on her plate.

"Good idea," Jonathan agreed.

Once they were finished with their supper and outside in the yard, Joe asked, "Which way shall we walk?"

"Down to the entrance of the tunnel first, before it gets dark," Mandie quickly told him.

"Mandie, you know that the door down there is locked, so what good will it do you to walk down there?" Jonathan asked.

"We can sit down for a few minutes when we get down there and plan out what we will do tomorrow while they are working on the tunnel, where we will sit so we can watch the entrance, and all that," Mandie quickly explained as she led the way down the hill.

She secretly never gave up the hope of finding the tunnel unlocked. She would never know until she went down and checked.

Chapter 10 / A Visitor

When Mandie and her friends opened the front door and went outside, Snowball had come running down the hall and slipped out with them.

Jonathan saw him and said, "Mandie, there is that white cat. Will he run away or get lost?"

Mandie smiled at him and replied, "No way. That cat knows every crack and corner of this property. And he may disappear for a while, but he always comes home. This is not like New York, where you have to keep your pets on a leash." She watched as Snowball ran ahead of them and disappeared down the hill.

"Now, Mandie, he has been lost a couple of times that I remember," Joe told her with a big smile.

"Yes, but that was unusual," Mandie said.

Celia suddenly stopped and said, "Oh, for good-ness' sake, I've caught my skirt on that rosebush." She was trying to reach the back of her dress, where it was stuck to a thorny branch.

"Hold still, I'll get it loose," Mandie told her and quickly came to remove the rosebush's thorns.

Celia tried to see the spot on the back of her skirt

where it had stuck. "I can't see. Did it damage my skirt?" she asked.

Mandie fluffed the material and stood back to look. "No, I can't even see where it was," she replied.

"Those big fluffy skirts you girls wear don't mix too well with rosebushes, do they?" Jonathan remarked.

"I shouldn't have been taking a shortcut through the rosebushes," Celia told him.

"Let's get back out on the main path," Mandie said, leading the way down the hill.

"Joe, you won't be here tomorrow because you are going off with Uncle Ned," Mandie remarked as they came out within sight of the bushes and trees hiding the entrance to the tunnel. "You may miss some excitement, depending on whether Uncle John opens up the crack or not."

"I realize that, but we need to get those chickens to Mrs. Fortner while we are here," Joe replied, walking beside her. "If he opens the crack, maybe we will get back in time to see what's behind it."

"But Mr. Shaw has not promised that we could go in and see whatever they find if they do open it," Jonathan said.

"Yes, and it could be something so dangerous that we won't be allowed in there at all," Celia added.

They came to the bushes, and Mandie quickly slipped through them to check the tunnel door. It was locked. She had known it would be. But then, you could never tell when someone might leave it unlocked. Stepping back to her friends, she said, "It's locked."

There was a slight crashing noise in the woods

nearby, and they all glanced at one another.

"Did you hear something?" Mandie asked as she quickly turned to look around toward the thicket nearby.

Joe and Jonathan pushed bushes back and ran in to search. They made a loud noise as they did.

"Whatever it was, y'all have scared it away with your racket," Mandie called to them as she watched to see if anything came out.

The boys returned to the clearing. Joe said, "Yes, we probably did. It might have been a squirrel or another animal."

"And those animals are always quicker than we are," Jonathan decided, stomping his feet to shake off the leaves that stuck to his pants.

"So are some human beings," Mandie added with a thoughtful frown.

"Anyhow, the tunnel door is locked, and if it was something or someone trying to get in there, they wouldn't have been able to," Celia reminded them.

"Oh well, let's go over here," Mandie said, leading the way through rhododendron bushes to the place where they had sat before.

When they were all seated, Joe looked in front of them and said, "You really can't see much from here except the door to the tunnel."

"And that means no one can see us if we just sit still and look and listen," Mandie reminded him.

"Do you think these workmen will come after breakfast?" Jonathan asked.

"We can get up early and eat breakfast in the kitchen before the others come downstairs," Mandie said.

"I imagine all the men will plan on doing that, because I would think they will all go to the tunnel with Mr. Shaw," Celia said.

"That would clutter up Aunt Lou's kitchen. What do you think she would have to say about that?" Jonathan asked with a grin.

Mandie looked at him and said, "She may not even be up early like we will."

"Now, how are we going to eat breakfast if there isn't any because Aunt Lou is not there to prepare it?" Jonathan asked.

"Oh, Jonathan, my uncle knows how to cook breakfast, and so do I," Mandie said and then added sadly, "I used to get up early when my father was living and we lived at Charley Gap. He always had the coffee made, and when I came down we would cook breakfast. He even knew how to make biscuits." Her eyes misted over as she remembered her father, Jim Shaw.

"What did your cook say about that?" Jonathan asked.

Everyone laughed at that remark. Mandie smiled at him and said, "We didn't have a cook, or any servants at all, and we lived in a log cabin, which, as you know, I still own. Those were happy days." She swallowed to keep her voice from shaking.

"Now, that would be wonderful, to be able to live without all those servants around, bossing everything all the time," Jonathan said with a big grin. "I think I'll marry you, Mandie Shaw, and live with you in that log cabin."

"Now, hold on just a minute," Joe quickly said. "That's taken care of already."

Mandie quickly stood up and said, "Let's walk back up the hill." Everyone followed without a word. She didn't want to get into the subject of marriage. Lifting her long skirts as she climbed uphill, she looked back at her friends and said, "Let's go out on the main road and walk for a while."

"Yes," they all agreed.

Once they were on the main road, they walked down into the business district. Most of the stores were closed for the night, but lots of people were strolling along the streets.

As they came to an intersection on Main Street, Mandie looked at Jonathan, laughed, and said, "And now here is Broadway."

Jonathan glanced around and said, "I don't believe New York's Broadway could have ever looked like this."

Different kinds of stores stood next to each other, with open parks here and there and benches in those. The structures were of a variety, some brick, some wooden, and some part mortar, some very old, some old, and some not so old. And most of the benches were unoccupied.

"Let's sit down over here for a few minutes," Mandie suggested as they came to a bench.

"I thought you wanted to walk," Joe said as he sat next to her and Jonathan and Celia joined them.

"I do, I did, and we will be walking back, and you know that involves some steep hills," Mandie replied. "I just thought we could catch our breath before doing that."

"Why, Mandie, you sound like you're getting old," Celia teased her.

"Oh no, not old, just curious about who is out for a walk besides us," Mandie said.

"You probably know everyone in town, don't you?" Jonathan asked. "After all, there aren't a whole lot of people living in Franklin."

"No, I don't know everyone in town," Mandie

replied. "You know I have only been living in Franklin for about three years, and most of that time I've been away to school in Asheville."

"Oh yes, I keep forgetting you lived over in Swain County near Joe when your father was living," Jonathan said.

Suddenly Mandie heard someone calling, "Missy 'Manda, Missy 'Manda, where you at?"

Mandie smiled at her friends as they all rose from the bench. "It's Liza." The girl had finally spotted her and was coming down the hill. "Here I am, Liza. What's wrong?"

"Aunt Lou, she send me to find you. Man at house wants to see you," Liza explained as soon as she could get her breath from running.

"A man at the house wants to see me?" Mandie questioned. "Who is it, Liza?"

"Lawsy mercy, Missy 'Manda, I disremember who dat man is," Liza replied. "Aunt Lou she say git a move on and git right back to de house. Come on now." She turned to go back up the road.

Mandie and her friends hurried after Liza.

"Must be a stranger if Liza doesn't know who he is," Joe remarked.

"Liza never is good at remembering people's names," Mandie said as they climbed the hill toward the house. Liza was way ahead of them and had disappeared into the house.

When they came within view of the house, Mandie saw a man sitting on the steps. The sun was fading, and she squinted to see who he was.

"Oh, it's Mr. Jacob Smith," she said excitedly.

"Yes, it is," Joe agreed.

"Who is Mr. Jacob Smith?" Jonathan asked as they hurried on.

"He lives in my father's house at Charley Gap," Mandie quickly explained.

As she came to the steps, the huge, burly, gray-haired man stood up and reached to embrace her with a tight squeeze. "And how is Jim Shaw's little daughter?" he asked.

"Oh, Mr. Jacob, I'm so glad to see you," Mandie told him as she held his hand. "You are like part of my past with my father." She blinked her eyes as she felt them mist over. Trying to control her feelings, she asked, "How are things with you, Mr. Jacob?"

"Just fine, just fine," he replied. "Got everything stocked up now to begin farming, thanks to the neighbors out there."

At that moment Liza pushed open the door, stuck her head out, and said loudly, "Aunt Lou say you git yo'selfs in dis heah house right now. She got coffee and choc'late cake awaitin'." She closed the door.

"Yes, ma'am," Mandie said with a big smile. Turning to her friends, she said, "We'd better get a move on, or Liza will be back."

When they went inside, Mandie went down the hall and opened the kitchen door and looked inside. Aunt Lou saw her and quickly said, "Now, y'all jes' take de comp'ny to de parlor. Liza gwine bring coffee and cake. Shoo now."

"But I thought maybe we could eat in here with you," Mandie protested.

"Dat ain't no way to treat dat friend of yo' pa's," Aunt Lou replied. She shook her white apron at Mandie and said, "Git now."

"Yes, ma'am, I'm going," Mandie said, and turning to her friends behind her, she said, "We have to go to the parlor and let Liza bring the coffee in there." She led the way to the parlor, where they sat down by the windows.

"Aunt Lou told me everyone was gone out to visit some friends and wouldn't be back until late," Jacob Smith said to Mandie.

"Yes, sir, they all went out together," Mandie explained. "And my mother didn't know when they'd be back, probably late, but you're going to spend the night, aren't you?"

"Well, I suppose I'll have to in order to see your uncle John," Mr. Smith replied.

Liza came in with the tea cart and began passing out the chocolate cake and coffee.

"You probably haven't heard, because Uncle John didn't want us to talk to people about it, but we have a crack in the wall of the tunnel under the house," Mandie told him.

Liza heard that remark and began grumbling as she finished serving the coffee. "Dis heah house might be gwine fall right down, might be," she said, just loud enough for everyone to hear.

"Now, Liza, this house is not going to fall in from that little crack in the tunnel," Jonathan said teasingly.

"Jes' you wait and see, wait and see," the girl replied as she left the room.

"A crack in the wall of the tunnel?" Mr. Smith questioned, drinking his coffee.

Mandie explained how they had all been in Charleston at the Pattons' house and Uncle Ned had come to tell Uncle John that he must go home to investigate the crack.

"But a crack in the wall of the tunnel wouldn't really be serious, would it?" Jacob Smith asked.

"I don't know how serious it is, but I saw it and there is something behind the crack, either a door or a wall," Mandie replied. "And I hope Uncle John finds out what it is before he seals up the crack."

"There's a possibility the crack was caused by the tornado that came through here back in the spring," Joe said. "So there could be more damage down there somewhere else."

Mandie quickly looked at Joe and said, "But Uncle John never mentioned anything like that. If there is more damage, then it could be awfully serious, couldn't it, Mr. Jacob?" She looked at Mr. Smith.

"Now, I couldn't rightly express any opinion on it because I have not seen the crack you are talking about. And I would have to make a thorough investigation of the whole tunnel to look for more damage," Mr. Smith told her.

"But Uncle John hasn't mentioned anything else down there. I don't know whether he has inspected the whole tunnel or not," Mandie said, looking at her friends. "Have y'all heard anyone mention doing that?"

"No, Mandie, I haven't heard anything," Celia said.

"Neither have I, but then, I haven't discussed it with my father and he has been down there with your uncle, Mandie," Jonathan told her.

Joe shrugged his shoulders and said, "I don't know any more than you do."

"The workmen have been going in and out the outside entrance to the tunnel, and we've been watching, but I don't know what my uncle will do about it," Mandie said and then added, "Would you like to see the outside entrance to the tunnel before it gets too dark, Mr. Jacob?"

"I could use a little walk," Mr. Smith said. "Been riding horseback nearly all day."

"Then let's walk down to the tunnel entrance," Mandie said, glancing at her friends.

Mandie knew her friends were tired of her going down to the tunnel entrance to check the door every time they went outside, so she was silent as they walked down the hill. Everyone else was quiet, too.

Just as they got within sight of the bushes hiding the tunnel door, Mandie heard someone talking, and she put up her hand and whispered to her friends, "Sh-h-h-h!" She crept forward, trying not to make a sound.

Everyone stopped where they were. As she got close enough to peek through the bushes, she was astonished to see Polly Cornwallis and that newspaperman messing with the lock on the door.

"I told you you couldn't unlock that door with pins. What a stupid idea," the reporter was saying.

"If I stick enough of them in the hole in the lock, it might work," Polly replied as she continued messing with the lock.

Mandie instantly hurried forward, pulled the bushes back, and confronted the two. "Just what are you doing, Polly Cornwallis? And you, reporter or cousin or whoever you are, my uncle has forbidden you to come on our property."

Mandie's friends and Jacob Smith had rushed forward when they heard the conversation between Mandie and the intruders.

"I was not doing anything," Polly argued, but then when she looked up and saw Mr. Smith, she quickly ran off into the bushes.

The reporter didn't budge. "I don't know why

you have to try to keep all this a secret, because it will surely be put in all the papers," he said.

"Don't you dare trespass on our property," Mandie said, walking up close to him.

Jacob Smith moved closer with her and asked, "Who are you, fella? This is private property."

Mandie looked up at him and explained, "He's that newspaper reporter that has been snooping around here. Uncle John told him never to come back."

"Then you had better get off this property immediately," Mr. Smith told him.

The reporter continued standing there as he said, "I'm not sure this is private property right here or that it belongs to the Shaws. Polly said it wasn't."

"I can guarantee you, buddy, this property does belong to the Shaws, and I myself will remove you if you don't get off it," Jacob Smith insisted, stepping nearer to the man.

The reporter drew in a long breath and then turned and ran off into the bushes.

"Shall we chase him, sir, to be sure he has gone?" Jonathan asked.

"I don't think he will return so long as he knows I am here," Mr. Smith replied.

Mandie walked over to the door of the tunnel and looked at the lock. "The lock is full of straight pins," she exclaimed as the others crowded around. "Polly has put straight pins in the lock."

"Let me see what I can do about this," Jacob Smith said, taking his pocketknife out of his pocket.

Mandie moved aside and watched as he carefully picked out the straight pins from the hole in the lock. Her friends joined her.

"What a dumb idea," Jonathan said, "thinking

she could unlock the door by sticking pins in the lock."

"All those pins could jam up the lock to where you couldn't unlock it with the key," Joe said.

"I figured all the time the pincushion belonged to Polly, but I had no idea she was using it for such a thing as this," Mandie remarked.

Mr. Smith got the last of the pins out and turned to ask, "Do you have the key? We could see if it works all right now or whether a pin or two might have slipped on down inside the lock."

Mandie shook her head and said, "No, Mr. Jacob, Uncle John has the key."

"Well, I don't think those two could open this lock without the key, so I'd say it's safe for now," Mr. Smith said.

They went back to the house and sat in the parlor until midnight, at which time the adults had still not returned and at which time everyone decided to go to bed. Aunt Lou showed Mr. Smith to a bedroom upstairs, and the young people went to their own rooms.

When Mandie and Celia got in bed, Celia immediately went to sleep. Mandie stayed awake thinking about the tunnel and about Polly and that reporter. She wanted to be up bright and early to tell her uncle about those two.

Chapter 11 / Preparations

Celia woke first the next morning. She leaned up on her elbow and shook Mandie. "You wanted to get downstairs early, didn't you, Mandie?" she asked.

"Mmmmm," Mandie grunted as she sat up in bed. And then remembering her reason, she quickly slid out of bed and hurried to get dressed. "Yes, I want to speak to Uncle John about Polly and that reporter."

Celia put on her clothes, and the two went down to the kitchen. There was no one there. The coffee was not made, either.

"Everybody must have overslept," Mandie said, going to pick up the percolator. "I'll get the coffee going." She took the can of coffee out of the cupboard and measured the amount to use. Dumping it into the coffeepot, she filled the pot with water and put it back on the stove.

"Mandie, the stove is hot. Someone must have been in here before us," Celia remarked as she held her hands near the hot iron stove door.

"You're right. It's hot enough to make the coffee," Mandie agreed. "But I wonder who built the fire in it? I don't think it could have been Uncle John or

Aunt Lou, because they would have made the coffee. But who could it have been?" She thought about it for a minute.

At that moment Uncle Ned came in the back door. "Good morning," he greeted them with a big smile. "I went for walk and came back to make coffee. You make coffee."

"Yes, sir, Uncle Ned, I just made it, and it ought to be ready by the time we get the cups," Mandie replied, going over to the cupboard and getting down cups and saucers.

John Shaw came into the kitchen from the hallway and said, "Now, that's nice of you, Amanda, to make the coffee."

Before she could reply, Joe and Jonathan also entered the room.

Mandie waited until everyone had coffee and they were seated at the table before she told John Shaw about Polly and the reporter.

"They both ran away when we caught them," she concluded.

Jacob Smith came in through the door from the hallway and joined them.

"Good morning. I didn't realize you were here," John Shaw greeted the man. "Pull out a chair and have some coffee."

"Thank you, that would be invigorating," Mr. Smith replied as he sat down and Mandie hurried to fill a cup with coffee for him.

"Oh, and Uncle John, I forgot to mention that Mr. Jacob was with us when we found Polly and that reporter down at the tunnel entrance," she said.

"I'm glad you were there," John Shaw told Jacob Smith. "Otherwise, Amanda and her friends might have had trouble with the two. I just don't know what I am going to do about them. Since Polly is a neighbor, I can't be too rude to her, but that reporter is absolutely trespassing. On the other hand, if I try to use legal means to keep him off the property, there's no telling what he might write in his newspaper about us. And I certainly don't want that tunnel publicized."

"That is a touchy situation," Jacob Smith agreed.

"We get braves watch property," Uncle Ned suggested. "Stop them from coming to tunnel."

"That would be a good solution, Uncle Ned," John Shaw told him. "Would you be able to get some young fellows over here today while we work on the crack?"

"Need go get chickens today," the old man said. "For Mrs. Fortner."

"I wonder if we could wait another day for that, Uncle Ned," John Shaw said. "I don't think it's real urgent, because she has plenty of chickens for the time being. In fact, it might be a couple more days before we could get the chickens, because I have decided to open up the crack, and that will take a much longer time than just repairing it."

Mandie grinned at her friends when they heard this.

Uncle Ned smiled at John Shaw and said, "Yes, right thing to open up crack. Chickens can wait. Braves coming today to help with filling crack. I tell them stand watch instead."

"Thank you, Uncle Ned, that will solve that problem, I believe," John Shaw said.

Jacob Smith spoke up. "I need to speak to you confidentially, John. I have a message to deliver."

John Shaw looked at him in surprise and asked,

"You do?" He stood up and said, "Suppose we step out in the yard, then, for a few minutes. The work-men will be here soon."

Mandie was listening, and she looked at her friends and saw they also had heard what Mr. Smith had to say. Now, what kind of a message did he have? And who was it from? she wondered as the two men left the room.

Joe grinned at her and said, "You will never hear what the message is."

"Maybe not now but later," Mandie answered. "He didn't tell us when he came last night that he had a message."

"But, Mandie, it was not a message for us. It was for your uncle," Celia reminded her.

"So why should he tell us that he had a mes-sage?" Jonathan asked.

"Well, I would like to know what the message is since it is considered so confidential," Mandie argued.

Uncle Ned spoke up. "Message not for Papoose," he said. "Must not pry."

Mandie took a deep breath and remained silent. She didn't want to argue with Uncle Ned. If John Shaw didn't allow the young people in the tunnel, she might be able to get some information about the crack from Uncle Ned.

John Shaw and Jacob Smith came back into the kitchen and sat down at the table. John Shaw told Mandie, "Whenever your grandmother comes downstairs, I need to speak to her, Amanda."

Now, this was getting to be a mystery. Whatever had been said between her uncle and Jacob Smith must concern her grandmother.

Jacob Smith drank up his coffee and said, "I

must be getting on the road home." He stood up.

"Do you have to leave now? We'll have some breakfast soon," John Shaw told him.

"No, I'd better not stay for breakfast. I usually don't eat much in the morning anyway. Besides, it won't take me long to get back to Charley Gap since I rode my horse and didn't bring the wagon," Jacob Smith replied. He looked down at Mandie and said, "Don't forget to come to see me, young lady."

"I'll come over one day before I go back to school," Mandie promised. "But I wish you could stay awhile."

"I've got work to do," he replied. "Maybe next time I can stay longer."

John Shaw walked out the back door with Jacob Smith as he went to get his horse from the barn. Uncle Ned followed.

Aunt Lou came into the kitchen from the hall door. She stopped, looked at everybody, and said, "Now, why didn't y'all let me know y'all up dis bright and early?" Going over to the stove, she opened the door to the firebox and added another piece of wood from the woodbox sitting behind the stove.

"We didn't want to bother you, Aunt Lou. I made the coffee," Mandie told her.

Aunt Lou looked at her and then opened the lid of the coffeepot. "Is it fittin' to be drunk?" she asked, bending to look inside the pot. She picked up the pot and carried it to the sink.

"Aunt Lou, don't pour it out. It tasted fine to me," Joe objected.

Aunt Lou looked at him and replied, "It mighta been, but it ain't now. Y'all done drunk it all up. Gotta make more." She dumped the coffee grounds into a can under the sink and began preparing another pot of coffee.

Liza came into the kitchen, rubbing her eyes and yawning.

Aunt Lou looked at Mandie and her friends. "Y'all drink up dat coffee in a hurry now and git out of heah," she said. "We'se got to git breakfast agoin'."

"Yes, ma'am," Mandie said, finishing the last of the coffee in her cup and standing up. Her friends joined her. "We'll leave now."

As the young people started for the back door, Mandie turned back to say, "Aunt Lou, if my grandmother comes down, Uncle John said he needs to speak to her."

"All right, git out of heah now," Aunt Lou replied.

The young people hurried out the back door. Mandie stopped on the back porch to look around. No one was in sight. Mr. Smith must have left, and Uncle John and Uncle Ned had probably gone down to the tunnel entrance.

"If we sit out there on the bench under that chestnut tree, we can see everybody going and coming to the tunnel entrance," she told her friends.

"And we won't be too far away to know when breakfast is ready," Jonathan added.

"Yes, that's important," Joe agreed.

"We couldn't go sit down near the tunnel entrance right now anyway because all the men are probably down there," Celia said.

Just as they got to the log bench and sat down, Uncle Ned came from around the front of the house. He had two young Cherokee men with him. They were speaking quickly in the Cherokee language and went on down the lane to the tunnel entrance without noticing Mandie and her friends.

"They must be the ones Uncle Ned said he would get to keep that reporter and Polly off our property," Mandie remarked.

"Probably," Joe said. "What I'd like to know is how they are going to do that. They certainly can't touch Polly, and y'all know she won't do anything she doesn't want to do."

"Yes, since she's a girl that's a problem," Jonathan said.

"Well, I'm a girl, too, and I'll help those Indians keep her away," Mandie told them.

"How, Mandie?" Celia asked.

Mandie thought for a minute and then said, "By scaring her. I'll tell her the house might fall in."

"And then she'll go tell that reporter and he'll put it in his paper that your house is in dangerous shape," Joe warned her.

"But his paper is all the way up in Raleigh," Mandie protested.

"And a lot of the people living here buy that Raleigh newspaper since that is the state capital," Joe replied.

"And your local newspaper would probably pick it up from the Raleigh paper," Celia added.

"I doubt that. Anyhow, we'll have the crack repaired before word could be circulated around about it," Mandie told them.

It wasn't long before John Shaw and Uncle Ned came up the hill from the tunnel entrance and went in the back door of the house. And then Liza came to get them for breakfast.

Mandie looked around the table. Everyone was present except her grandmother. Where could she be? She had hoped to hear whatever it was Uncle

John was going to tell Mrs. Taft, but she wasn't there and no one mentioned her name. Senator Morton was there. He was sitting next to Jane Hamilton.

"Have you noticed?" Mandie whispered to her friends at the table. "My grandmother isn't here."

"Probably just sleeping late," Jonathan decided.

"Maybe she'll be along shortly," Joe suggested.

"I hope she isn't sick," Celia said.

"Sick?" Mandie questioned. She had not even thought of such a thing. Her grandmother was never sick. She could outdo everyone else when she wanted to.

Then suddenly the door opened, and Mrs. Taft came hurrying into the room and took a seat on the other side of Senator Morton.

"I apologize for being late," she said, looking around the table. "I had to do some things before I came downstairs."

Liza immediately came to Mrs. Taft's side with the coffeepot and filled her cup. "Would you like fo' me to fill up dat plate fo' you?" Liza asked.

"Oh yes, that would be nice, Liza, please," Mrs. Taft replied. "Just give me a dab of grits and a little bacon and eggs. That would be fine."

"Yessum," Liza said, picking up Mrs. Taft's plate and taking it to the sideboard, where she proceeded to pile it high with food.

When she brought it back, Mrs. Taft looked at it in surprise, frowned, and then smiled. "Thank you, Liza," she said as she picked up her fork and began eating.

"I don't think my grandmother will eat all that food," Mandie told her friends, almost giggling behind her hand.

"Liza must have figured she was hungry," Jonathan whispered.

John Shaw was seated across the table from Mrs. Taft. He laid down his fork and spoke to her. "After we finish the meal, Mrs. Taft, may I have a word with you?"

Mrs. Taft looked at him in surprise and replied, "Of course, John."

Mandie whispered behind her hand to her friends, "Uncle John hasn't told her whatever it is yet."

Her friends shook their heads and looked at Mrs. Taft.

Mandie tried to listen to the grown-ups' conversation, but she could only hear snatches of it now and then.

"It will be after noontime before we can tell," John Shaw told Jane Hamilton in answer to a question that Mandie could not understand.

"Please be careful down there, John," Elizabeth cautioned him.

"I am not involved in the work myself. Those young Cherokee men are doing most of it, with Cliff supervising," John Shaw replied.

"You are not allowing anyone else in there, are you?" Elizabeth asked, slightly glancing at Mandie and her friends.

Mandie immediately dropped her eyes and hurriedly forked up her food, pretending she had not heard a word.

"Of course not. Everyone has been warned not to go inside the tunnel," John replied.

Dr. and Mrs. Woodard were seated next to Elizabeth, and Mandie saw the doctor glance down the table at them.

"I think everyone realizes how dangerous it could be if that wall caves in when they open the crack," Dr. Woodard said.

After that the adults' conversation turned to other things.

Finally the meal was over, and everyone began leaving the room. Mandie noticed Uncle John motioning to Mrs. Taft to follow him into the hallway and tried to follow closely behind them. Her uncle walked on down the hallway, though, and waited for Mrs. Taft to catch up with him.

"Come on, Mandie," Celia said as Mandie stopped outside the dining room door and watched. "You can't follow them."

"No, but I can watch from here," Mandie whispered to her friends as she moved slowly across the hall. They followed.

The other adults moved on down the hallway to the parlor. Mandie and her friends stood there, whispering to each other, with Mandie looking down the corridor at her grandmother and John Shaw.

Whatever her uncle was telling her grandmother seemed to be a surprise to the lady. She threw up her hands as she quickly replied and shook her head. Then she hurried down the hallway to the parlor and went in. John Shaw followed her.

"Come on," Mandie told her friends and hurried after the adults.

When she and her friends entered the parlor, Mandie saw her grandmother talking to her mother. But she couldn't get close enough to overhear the conversation. The young people sat down as near to the adults as they could find seats, but it was too far away in the huge room to overhear conversations.

Liza had brought the tea cart in and was serving

the coffee. As she passed Mandie, she whispered, "Yo' grandma she gwine home, ain't she?"

Mandie looked at her in surprise and replied, "I don't know. Did something happen to cause her to have to go home?"

"Now, dat's whut I'm askin' you, Missy 'Manda," Liza said. "I only hears her say she's gwine git packed and be ready to leave tomorrow. Now, don't dat sound like she be gwine home?"

"Yes, Liza, it does, but I don't know anything about it," Mandie said. "Who did she say that to?"

"She be tellin' yo' ma," Liza replied, hurriedly leaving the room.

Mandie looked at her friends, who had overheard the conversation with Liza. "Something must be wrong at her home," she told them.

"She will probably tell you all about it before she leaves," Joe said.

"And I suppose the senator will go with her," Jonathan said. "Looks like no chance for my father there."

Mandie grinned at him and said, "That's right."

Mandie was anxious to walk down to the tunnel entrance and watch from there to see what was going on, but she also wanted to know what was happening with her grandmother, and she couldn't be in two places at one time.

Finally Mandie heard Mrs. Taft suggest to Senator Morton that they go for a walk. And she couldn't follow them, so she decided to go on down to the tunnel entrance.

"Let's go sit in our special place down at the tunnel and watch what goes on down there," Mandie told her friends.

"I'll go, but I don't think we will be able to see

anything that goes on because all the activity will be inside the tunnel," Joe told her.

"You never know what might happen, though," Mandie replied.

"We might be able to ask the workmen some questions," Jonathan said.

"They may not speak English," Joe told him.

"Let's go find out," Mandie said.

They would sit there near the tunnel entrance and try to find out what was going on inside the tunnel.

Chapter 12 / The Past

Mandie and her friends watched and managed to get down near the tunnel without the adults seeing them. They sat in the place half hidden by the bushes, where no one could walk by them but from where they could see people going in and out of the tunnel.

"I don't see Uncle Ned's friends who are supposed to be watching the tunnel," Joe said, looking around the area.

"Oh, they are never seen but they can see you. You know how secretive they are about things like that," Mandie told him.

"There are some men in the tunnel working, I suppose," Jonathan said.

"There should be," Mandie agreed.

"Too bad we didn't get down here in time to see who all went in there," Jonathan said.

"I think the only people working in there are the Cherokee man, Cliff, and his Cherokee friends," Mandie said.

"I'd like to know what they are doing," Jonathan remarked.

"Yes, and I'd also like to know what is going on

with my grandmother," Mandie said. "Something is going on, and I haven't figured out yet what it is." She frowned as she thought about the conversation between Mrs. Taft and John Shaw, the part that she could hear. And what did Jacob Smith have to do with it all? He had been her father's friend, and she didn't believe her grandmother had even known him.

Joe looked at Mandie and said, "I know what you are thinking. What is the connection between Mrs. Taft and Mr. Jacob Smith?"

Mandie looked at him in surprise. "Why yes, I can't imagine what happened this morning. Evidently Mr. Jacob gave Uncle John a message for my grandmother, but what message was it? Not only that, how did Mr. Jacob know my grandmother was here?"

"Knowing Mandie Shaw, I'd say we'll have that mystery solved sooner or later," Jonathan said with a big grin.

"It must be something awfully important for Mr. Smith to come all the way over here to tell her whatever it is," Celia remarked.

"What do y'all plan on doing the rest of the summer? My grandmother wants us to go home with her, but I'm not sure I want to," Mandie said.

"I suppose I'll leave it up to my mother about what I should do," Celia said.

Snowball, Mandie's white cat, came running down the hill and went straight to them and jumped up in Mandie's lap.

"Well, Snowball, what's the hurry?" Mandie asked as she stroked his fur. "Something must have scared him."

"Like a dog?" Jonathan asked.

"No, not a dog. Snowball chases dogs, believe it or not," Mandie replied. Snowball jumped back down and ran off through the bushes. "He may be playing around with a squirrel."

"Squirrels can hurt," Celia said. "They have sharp teeth."

"I hear someone coming down the hill," Mandie whispered.

The four sat silently waiting to see who would appear through the bushes as the footsteps came closer.

"Sh-h-h-h! It's Uncle John and Uncle Ned," Mandie whispered.

The four sat completely still, waiting and watching.

"I just want to be sure the men don't need anything before I leave," John Shaw was saying. "I won't be gone long, but in case anyone shows up around here, be sure your men get rid of them, Uncle Ned."

"Braves watch; no one come near," the old Indian said.

The two men entered the tunnel. Mandie couldn't hear anything after that. But then, the workmen were a long distance up in the tunnel, and it would be impossible to hear them from the entrance.

The young people waited silently. Finally John Shaw and Uncle Ned came back out of the tunnel.

"Looks like it will be quite a while before they get enough of the wall out to see what's behind the crack. I'll be back by then," John Shaw said as they started to walk up the hill.

"Yes, go slow so wall not fall in," Uncle Ned said as they went on.

Once they were out of sight, Mandie said, "I wish

I could see what's going on in there."

The four sat there engrossed with their own thoughts for a long time. Snowball didn't return, and there was no sound coming from the tunnel. No one came down the hill. Everything was silent.

Suddenly there was loud talking in the tunnel, and Cliff and the two young Cherokee men came rushing outside, speaking loudly in Cherokee. The two young men ran up the hill, and Cliff went after them.

"They must be having some kind of argument," Mandie said.

"It certainly sounded like it," Jonathan said.

"Their language sounds so much different from ours that it's hard to figure out what they are saying," Joe remarked.

"They were the only ones in the tunnel, weren't they?" Celia asked.

Mandie sat up straight and said, "Yes, they were. I am going to look while they are gone." She stood up.

"And I'll go with you," Jonathan said, also rising.

"Mandie, I don't think you ought to go inside. Your uncle will be furious if you are caught in there," Joe reminded her.

"Yes, Mandie, I wouldn't go in there," Celia added.

"It will only take me a couple of minutes to run down the tunnel and see what they've done," Mandie insisted.

She hurried off into the entrance of the tunnel. Jonathan followed.

The men had left lanterns sitting here and there along the way so it was not dark. She could see nothing unusual as she went along, inspecting the walls as she got deeper inside the tunnel. Then up ahead she could see a whole lot of lanterns lighting up the place and knew instantly that was where the crack was.

"Here's the crack," she whispered to Jonathan, who was following. She saw when she got closer that the crack was a lot wider than when she had seen it before. Debris was piled up nearby.

"They have started widening it," she told Jonathan.

Jonathan got close to the wall to try and see what was on the other side. Mandie picked up one of the lanterns and flashed it along the wall. The light faintly illuminated the opening.

"Jonathan, there is something behind this crack," she said excitedly. She pressed her face against the mortar. Then she stood back and looked at the crack. "You know, Jonathan, I believe I can get through that crack and see what is on the other side if you will hold the lantern for me."

"Mandie, you are not going through that small space," Jonathan said. "You might get stuck, and I don't know how I would get you out."

"If I can get through without getting stuck, then I can get back out without getting stuck," she insisted, handing him the lantern. "Hold this up close for me so it won't be so dark in there when I get through. And, Jonathan, don't you dare run off and leave me in there."

"I won't, Mandie, but I still don't think you ought to try it," Jonathan replied, holding the lantern up close to inspect the crack. "The wall could start crumbling because they have been working on it and have probably loosened a lot of mortar."

"Just hold the lantern still and let me see if I can

get through," Mandie insisted as she quickly wrapped her full skirt around her tightly and put one foot through the crack. She turned sideways and practically held her breath as she managed to squeeze her torso, her head, and finally her other foot through the crack.

"Mandie, please be careful," Jonathan told her. "There could be some creatures living in there."

"Jonathan, don't say that," Mandie screeched back to him. "I'm in here now, anyway. Hold the lantern up to the crack and let me see if I can figure out what's in here."

Jonathan held the lantern against the crack and waited.

Mandie squinted her eyes to see better and then told Jonathan, "This is a room, a real room, Jonathan, and—" Suddenly she tried to scream and couldn't, and in a hoarse whisper she told him, "There's a grave in here, Jonathan. Help me to get out. Quick!" She backed away from the nearby mound of dirt with a head marker and tried to put her foot back through the crack. She was trembling with fright so badly she couldn't manage to squeeze back through.

"Come on, Mandie," Jonathan told her excitedly. "Put your foot through or something; come on and get out of there." He tried to reach through the small opening.

Mandie was shaking so hard she couldn't concentrate on what she was doing. Finally Jonathan gave up. "Mandie, I'll leave the lantern right here next to the crack," he said. "I'm going to get Joe to help."

"Don't leave me alone in here," Mandie cried as he ran off down the tunnel.

He came back with Joe and Celia in a few minutes that seemed like hours to Mandie.

"Mandie, where are you?" Joe asked as he picked up the lantern and flashed its light through the crack.

"Mandie, come on out," Celia called to her.

"Joe, help me," Mandie called out from the other side of the wall. "There's a grave in here." Her voice broke.

Joe stooped down, picked up a chisel the men had been using, and started to work trying to widen the crack.

"I'll help," Jonathan said, picking up another chisel and hammering on the crack with it.

Mortar began to fall everywhere as the boys pounded, and the crack gradually grew wider.

"Mandie, try it now. I think you can squeeze through," Joe told her. "Reach through and give me your hand."

Mandie reached for his hand and said, "Everybody, our verse." All four friends instantly joined hands as they repeated their favorite Bible verse, "What time I am afraid I will put my trust in Thee."

"Now," Mandie said and began pushing through the crack. The release was so sudden she practically fell into the arms of Joe and Jonathan, who kept her from ending up on the rough cement floor. She sat down, shaking with fright.

"Mandie, are you all right?" Joe asked as he stooped by her side.

"Come on, Mandie, let's get out of here," Celia told her.

Jonathan flashed the lantern light through the crack, which was much wider now, and excitedly said, "Mandie was right. There is a grave in there."

Joe bent forward from Mandie's side to look. "Yes, there is," he said.

Mandie got to her feet and said, "Let's get the crack open enough to see exactly what is in there."

"Sit back down there. Jonathan and I will widen it if we can," Joe told her.

Mandie collapsed again on the cement floor, and Celia sat by her. The two boys chipped and hammered at the crack, and it suddenly gave way in large chunks, exposing the room behind it. The boys stood back and looked.

Mandie got to her feet and said, "See, I told you there was a grave in there." She pointed through the large opening.

Joe stepped through and inspected the grave. There was a post for the head marker, with an army cap hanging on it. He stooped to pick it up and examine it. A folded paper fell out of it.

"Look, Mandie, there is a piece of paper in this hat," he said, holding the paper out to her as she stood watching.

Taking the paper, Mandie's trembling hands managed to unfold it. She squinted in the light of the lantern to read the contents. The others crowded close by and held lanterns to illuminate.

She read, " 'Here lies Corporal Albert McKinnon from Washington, who attempted to kill me because I would not give up my Cherokee friends to be removed from their land to Oklahoma. My dear friend, Wirt Pindar, shot him and saved my life. May the Lord have mercy on this soldier's soul. Signed, John Shaw, Senior.' "

Mandie was completely still and silent for a moment as the importance of what she held finally soaked through to her. Her friends waited and watched.

"This is signed by my father's father, my grandfather. And Uncle Wirt shot this man," she managed to say as the paper shook in her hands.

Joe reached over, took the paper, folded it, and put it in his pocket. "Come on, Mandie, we need to get out of here," he said.

"Yes, let's hurry," Celia added, shivering all over.

Jonathan moved over to hold Celia's hand. "It's all over now. It's just a grave in there. Let's go."

Celia allowed Jonathan to move her along the tunnel toward the entrance. Joe and Mandie followed.

They were about one-third of the way out when John Shaw and Uncle Ned came rushing in and almost knocked them down before they saw them.

"Amanda! What are you doing in here?" John Shaw demanded.

Mandie looked up through tears and couldn't reply. Joe pulled out the paper and handed it to John Shaw.

"What is this?" the man asked as he quickly unfolded it. Then as he read it, he exclaimed, "So there is a grave in there, and my father must have had it sealed up to protect his friends." He hurried on down the tunnel toward the crack after he explained to Uncle Ned what the paper said.

The young people turned and came along behind him and Uncle Ned. The two men were conversing in the Cherokee language, and Mandie and her friends couldn't understand a word they were saying. She remembered that her uncle's mother had been full-blooded Cherokee. Therefore, he would know the language.

John Shaw and Uncle Ned took several lanterns into the hidden room and explored the walls.

"Look here, Uncle Ned," John Shaw said, pointing to a wall where he stood. "There's a dumbwaiter here, and it has been sealed off upstairs." He pointed overhead. "See that patching on the ceiling there?"

"Yes," the old Indian said. "What do now, John Shaw?"

John Shaw thought for a moment and then said, "My father said Uncle Wirt shot this man and saved his life by doing so, but I think we need to keep this quiet and just seal the room back up, the way he had done it. What do you think?"

"Yes, we tell Wirt but we tell no one else," Uncle Ned said.

"We will go back to the house now, Amanda, and none of this is to ever be discussed with anyone outside the family by any of you," John Shaw said, looking at Mandie and her friends.

"No, sir," Joe said instantly.

Jonathan nodded his head. "I won't talk about it."

"I certainly won't," Celia added.

"Let's get the men back in here and close it," John Shaw said as they walked down the tunnel toward the exit.

When they got back to the house, John Shaw called everyone together in the parlor and told them the story.

"I trust no one will ever repeat this outside of this room," he ended up saying. "That's mainly to protect Uncle Wirt, and it is our own private business."

Senator Morton, Mrs. Taft, Mr. Guyer, Jane Hamilton, Dr. and Mrs. Woodard, Jason Bond, the caretaker, who had just returned from his errand for John Shaw, Uncle Ned, Elizabeth Shaw, and the four young people all listened and agreed.

"The men will reseal the crack with something stronger than what's there and repair it so it will not be noticeable. Therefore future generations of Shaws who live in this house will have no reason to suspect there's a room back there," John Shaw explained. "And Uncle Ned has the workmen sworn to secrecy because of Uncle Wirt."

When the meeting was over, Mandie said to her friends, "Let's sit on the back porch for a little while." She needed some fresh air badly.

After they had all sat down, the door opened and Mandie looked up to see her grandmother standing there.

"Are you going to join us, Grandmother?" Mandie asked.

"No, dear, I thought perhaps you all would join me," Mrs. Taft said. She stopped and looked at each one.

"Join you? Where?" Mandie asked.

"At my house in Asheville, dear," Mrs. Taft said. "Before you decide, I must tell you the news."

The four young people instantly straightened up to listen.

"You all know Mr. Jacob Smith, I'm sure," Mrs. Taft said as she looked directly at Mandie.

"Yes, ma'am," replied the four.

"Well, Mr. Smith brought me a message," Mrs. Taft continued and then paused.

Mandie quickly smiled and thought, *She's going to tell us what it was.*

"It seems that we have an awfully big mystery back in Asheville," Mrs. Taft said. "And several people there had to trace me down. Mr. Smith happened to be in Asheville and knew where I was."

Mandie thought, *Oh, please hurry up and tell us what the mystery is.*

"Girls, Miss Hope at your school has completely disappeared, not a sign of her anywhere now for three days before Mr. Smith came," Mrs. Taft explained.

The four drew in their breath.

"Miss Hope missing?" Mandie said. "Oh, I hope nothing has happened to her."

"Yes, Miss Hope is nice," Celia added.

"And it's the other one, her sister, Miss Prudence, who is so tough on you girls, isn't it?" Joe asked.

The girls nodded.

"Now, since I own the school, Miss Prudence has sent me this news and asked if I could launch a search for her sister, and I thought perhaps you young people might want to help," she said, looking around the group.

"Oh, yes, ma'am, Grandmother," Mandie instantly replied.

"Yes," Celia agreed. "That is, if my mother will allow me to go to Asheville with y'all."

"And I want to go, also, but I'll have to clear it with my father," Jonathan said.

"I'll go with you," Joe promised.

"I thank you all," Mrs. Taft said. "Now, we need to get that train out of here tomorrow, so please be ready." She went back inside.

The young people discussed the newest mystery. Where was Miss Hope? She was shy, and it wasn't like her to just disappear without letting anyone know where she was going.

Mandie thought, *But we'll find you, Miss Hope. I know we will.*

So they were all going home to Asheville with Mrs. Taft after all.

COMING NEXT!

MANDIE AND THE MISSING SCHOOLMARM
(Mandie Book/39)

Miss Hope has suddenly disappeared.
Where could she be?
Mandie and her grandmother launch a search.
What has happened to the lovable schoolmarm?